THE ULTIMATE EXAM

"The five of you will be set loose in the jungle terrain beyond our fortress," Hammerlock said. "I'll give you until dawn and then start after you. I think that's a sporting chance.

"I'll probably be back in time for breakfast, but it would be a pleasant surprise if you were tough enough to make the hunt last until lunch."

Hammerlock drew his Super Blackhawk pistol. He twirled the gun about his forefinger. "Just consider this the final exam."

Suddenly Hammerlock stopped the spinning gun. It was pointed right at Joe's head.

"And I mean just that. You flunk this course—and you die!"

D0189238

Books in THE HARDY BOYS CASEFILES® Series

Available from ARCHWAY Paperbacks

THE HARDY BOYS CASEFILES NO. 7

DEATHGAME

FRANKLIN W. DIXON

AN ARCHWAY PAPERBACK
Published by POCKET BOOKS
New York   London   Toronto   Sydney   Tokyo

AN ARCHWAY PAPERBACK *Original*

An Archway Paperback published by
POCKET BOOKS, a division of Simon & Schuster, Inc.
1230 Avenue of the Americas, New York, N.Y. 10020

ISBN: 0-671-62648-5

First Archway Paperback printing September 1987

10 9 8 7 6 5 4 3

Printed in the U.S.A.

IL 7+

DEATHGAME

Chapter

1

"JOE, I CAN'T believe I let you talk me into this."
Frank Hardy glared at his younger brother, Joe.
Then his eyes went to the gun clenched in his own
hand. "It's crazy and—"

"Keep it down, will you!" Even in a whisper,
Joe Hardy's voice was sharp. He nodded toward
the area beyond the thick bushes that concealed
them. "One of the guys out there will hear you."

Frank peered into the early-evening dusk, trying to catch any trace of movement in the dark
woods. The air was full of nighttime sounds:
crickets, wind beating against the upper branches
of the trees, the occasional buzz of a mosquito
seeking blood.

Beyond the woods, the Hardys could hear
waves battering the rocky cliffs at the Bayport

1

inlet. Half-seen in the shadows, an overgrown path twisted serpent-fashion through the woods, past bushes and rocks.

Joe Hardy checked the load in his pistol. It was exactly like Frank's weapon. Satisfied, Joe cautiously closed the chamber and let his eyes scan the path.

He could see no movement. Still, he knew they were out there, waiting to close in for the kill.

In the shadows Joe could see his eighteen-year-old brother running a hand through his brown hair—a sure sign that Frank was nervous. Joe thought the whole thing was turning into a lot more than he had bargained for. Here it was, a warm Saturday night in July. Joe could have been at a movie, having fun. Instead, he was sweating in the woods, waiting to kill or be killed.

Joe's eyes went back to the trail. It was too dark to see. He'd have to rely on sounds: a snapped twig, leaves brushing against clothes. All he had to do was listen for that one out-of-place noise.

"Come on, Frank, this will be a piece of cake," Joe whispered, trying to reassure himself. "They don't realize who they're up against. We're practically professionals."

Like Joe, Frank was crouched behind a low bush. He stirred, irritated. "The reason we're so good is because I take nothing for granted. So be quiet. I want—"

He stopped as they both heard a loud snap.

"That's them!" Joe whispered tensely. He strained his eyes, staring toward a rise where the trail curled around a boulder covered with lichens. Joe saw something move near the rock. Could it have been just a branch or—no!

A hand.

A hand holding a pistol.

No mistake.

The hunter had pressed himself against the jagged rock at the rise in the trail. His body almost blended in perfectly with his cover. He seemed content to remain where he was.

"See him?" Joe murmured to Frank.

"I'm not blind," Frank whispered. "But where's his friend?"

Where *was* the hunter's partner? On the trail? Creeping up behind them? Joe's skin crawled at the thought of being shot in the back.

Rising from his cover, Joe dashed for the dense woods a few feet away.

Frank didn't question his brother's move. "I'll cover you," he whispered, raising the barrel of his gun.

Joe made his way through the trees, dropping behind his brother. Now to circle around, so I can come out onto the trail behind the hunter, Joe thought, ducking under branches. Every now and then he heard a suspicious noise, paused, and then moved on. The breeze was working for the enemy that night.

Joe eased out of the woods. He was closing in

on the rock where his quarry was hiding. Only a few more steps, and he would be ready to nail him.

That was when he saw the second hunter. Like the first one, he was a large male dressed in black. And he had risen out of the underbrush only a few feet from Frank. Joe could see a glint of silver over the hunter's eyes. That meant he was wearing special night-vision goggles.

Joe had to do something to save Frank! But he was too far away for a clear shot. He thought of screaming to confuse the predator, but that would warn the hunter near the boulder; he'd shoot Joe dead in a second. Joe began to breathe faster, awaiting the inevitable.

Frank Hardy held his breath as he heard the telltale rustle of brush. Close. *Too* close. He squeezed the handle of his pistol. Could it be Joe? No, Frank had no idea where his brother was, but he did know he was being watched by *hostile* eyes. He must move, whatever the cost.

Frank dove backward toward the trail, branches whipping past his face. He heard Joe shout, "Frank!"

Almost immediately he heard a shot. Something ripped through the bushes where he had just been.

After Frank landed on the path, he came up into a crouch. Immediately, the person who had molded himself to the rock jumped out and rushed toward him, shooting as he ran. Someone else was moving rapidly through the trees in Frank's direction.

Frank whipped his pistol toward the first attacker, firing two quick shots. That ended the charge. The guy made an awkward about-face and scuttled back to the safety of his jagged rock. Another shot sounded from farther away. *Joe*. The unlucky attacker hugged the ground.

Frank felt safe for only a moment. The second attacker was gaining on him quickly, and Frank was an easy target on the path.

He leapt to his feet and started running through the woods toward the sound of the crashing surf. Once free of the woods, he could find a hiding place among the craggy cliffs and wait for his pursuers. He would have more of a chance against them there. He knew the terrain above the beach as well as anyone.

It took Frank two minutes of hard running before he came to a bank of huge boulders at the top of the Bayport cliffs that edged down to the Atlantic. Waves smashed onto the rocks far below him.

He knelt beside a boulder, looking toward the woods. Feathery clouds, pushed by the gathering wind, slid across a half-moon. He held his gun ready.

Frank was calm now. He could hear someone running through the woods. In a few seconds, whoever it was would come out into the open and be caught in his gunsight.

He sensed victory and waited eagerly for his pursuer.

"Hey, Frank Hardy. Guess what?" a voice asked sarcastically. Three feet behind Frank, the leader stood up. "You lose," he said coldly, and pulled the trigger of his gun.

Frank fell backward on the rocks.

The leader approached slowly, his gun still aimed at Frank's body. He pulled off the infrared goggles, checking his kill.

An indisputable kill, marked by a splash of shocking red spreading over Frank Hardy's chest, its center directly over his heart!

Chapter

2

JOE HARDY BURST from the woods, his pistol ready. He came to an abrupt stop when he saw Frank.

His brother lay on the rocks, a black-clad figure standing over him. A second figure came to a halt close to Joe and whirled, gun in hand.

Joe turned and snapped off a shot without even glancing to see where he had hit the guy. He was too busy bringing his gun to bear on the leader.

"Too late, Joe. It's all over."

The leader's gun had already covered Joe. The first pellet splattered against his gun hand. A second pellet burst against his knee, and the third hit dead center in his stomach. Three shots in as many seconds. There was red gel everywhere.

"How's that for fancy shooting?" The black-clad figure whipped off his goggles, laughing. Biff Hooper slapped his goggles against his thigh. His initials, B.H., glinted silver where they were inscribed near the edge of the octagonal lenses.

"Show-off!" Joe grumbled, dropping his gun.

"You can get up now, Frank," Biff said in a mocking tone.

Frank sat up, a disgusted look on his face. He ran a hand through the red goo on his chest.

"You're a real mess, Frank," Biff said, helping him to his feet.

"You said the paint in those pellets would wash out," Frank said, staring at the red goop on his hand. "If it doesn't come off, I'll be after you for real."

Tony Prito shook his head as he walked over to Joe. "Well, you got me, Joe, if it makes you feel any better," Tony said. His fingers touched a red smear through his dark hair. He looked about as happy as Frank. With a shrug he headed back toward the woods.

Biff walked jauntily over to Joe. "Cheer up, Hardy. You took my challenge to a survival game and you lost. Too bad you were up against the master."

Throwing an arm around Joe, Biff patted his shoulder in an ironic gesture of comfort. "And don't sweat my telling everybody that I outdid you guys. I've got class. I know how to win."

"Oh, great," said Frank. He glared at Joe. "How'd I let you talk me into this stupid game?"

"Hey!" Biff protested. "It is *not* stupid. It's a sport that takes skill, patience, daring, and strategy! There are professional camps all over the country for it. And I bet I could turn up at any of them and come home a winner."

"Let's get back to where we parked the cars," Frank said curtly. He stopped for a second to scoop up some leaves to wipe his hands on.

Joe stopped beside Frank. "You just didn't take it seriously," he growled. "If you hadn't been complaining all the time, we'd have beaten them."

"Not a chance!" Biff said, laughing and twirling his gun in three quick flips.

Biff was blond and stood well over six feet. His wide shoulders looked as if they'd have trouble passing through a doorway. His chest was almost as wide, layered with muscles from working out. He was friendly, quick to smile, and usually easygoing. Only on the football field had Joe seen the tough competitiveness that lay beneath the nice-guy exterior.

At least, that was how he'd been before his new interest in survival games. Joe had to admit that that night Biff hadn't been playing like a nice guy. He'd better control that aggressive streak, Joe thought. It could get him into trouble.

Fenton Hardy always told his sons that analyzing personality was as important as gathering physical evidence in solving crimes. That was how he had become a top private investigator.

Joe liked to think that reading people was his specialty while high-tech information gathering was Frank's strong point. And watching the new Biff rang warning bells in Joe's head.

"You know, this game wasn't really on the level," Joe said as he started to trail after his brother into the woods.

"How do you figure that?" Biff asked.

"Well, you had those special night-vision goggles. They gave you an edge."

"I just call that being prepared," Biff said with a grin.

"You're overdoing it, Hooper." Joe shook his head.

Biff grabbed his arm. "Hey, Joe? Can you hold up a minute?"

Biff's voice was suddenly quiet. Joe turned around. "Everything okay?" he asked.

Biff unsnapped the pouch on his utility belt that held his initialed goggles. His eyes didn't meet Joe's. "I can't tell Frank this. You know how he is," Biff whispered. He looked vulnerable, anything but the tough victor of that night's survival game.

The other two were far ahead, walking through the dark to the road. Joe could hear them laughing. He stood patiently, listening to the waves break while Biff decided to tell him whatever was on his mind.

"See, I buy these survival game magazines," Biff began. "They have ads for seminars. You go someplace in the wilderness and play the game for two or three days. There's this one place that sounds really fantastic."

"So?" Joe asked.

"So, it's called the Ultimo Survival Camp. It's kind of far away and expensive, but I think I'm going to go."

"Where is it, Australia?"

"Not that far. It's in Georgia. The nearest town is called Clayton," Biff said.

"How much does it cost?" Joe asked.

"Well, let's just say that I'll have to mow a lot of lawns when I get back to make my savings account healthy again," he said. "But how can you beat a survival camp at a place called Screamer Mountain?"

Joe realized that as Biff spoke, he was trying to convince himself that going to the camp would be okay.

"I'm sick of hanging around Bayport," Biff said abruptly. "You have your detective thing, so I thought you might understand. This is a chance to have some real adventure in my life." He grabbed Joe's arm. "I'm going tomorrow. I'll be back in three days."

"You aren't going to tell your parents, are you?" Joe asked, understanding at last.

"No, you're the only one who knows, and you've got to keep it a secret. I've told my mom and dad that I'm going to visit my aunt and uncle near Albany."

Joe shook his head. "I don't think this is a great idea, but I won't rat on you," he said. "Just be back in three days."

"Sure—I will." Biff sounded excited now, as if his plan seemed more real for having confided it. "Remember—don't tell Frank."

"I won't," Joe said. And they ran to catch up with the others.

"Do you know where he's gone?" demanded the voice over the phone. "It's been four days. We've tried everything. Please, if you know anything, you must help us."

Mrs. Hooper sounded as if she was close to hysteria. Joe Hardy felt a sick emptiness in his stomach. Something had happened to Biff at the Ultimo Survival Camp, and Biff's parents didn't have a clue as to where their son was.

"We thought he'd gone to my brother's place upstate," Mrs. Hooper's voice shook. "That's what he told us, but—but he didn't. When he didn't come back in three days, we called—and he had never been there. This is turning into a nightmare."

Joe took a deep breath. "I think I may know where he is," he said simply. He told Mrs. Hooper everything Biff had confided in him—which he realized wasn't all that much.

Georgia in July was hot, very hot.

Joe and Frank sat on either side of Biff's father

in the back of a black-and-white police car. Mr. Hooper was a tall, slender man, not given to showing emotion. He sat silently, dabbing at his perspiring forehead with a handkerchief. Biff's mother sat in the front, her blond hair awry. She was silent, too.

Sheriff Kraft, from the town of Clayton, drove them over the dirt road that cut through the lush, low mountains. Periodically, he would try to start a conversation, without success. The air-conditioning in his car was broken, but he didn't seem to mind a bit.

Frank Hardy studied his brother's set face. Joe usually wasn't so quiet. He'd been like that once before—when Iola Morton, his girlfriend, had died in a car bombing. He feels guilty, Frank realized. He knows he should have tried to talk Biff out of going but he didn't.

Joe ignored the hot wind blowing in the window. What if he were responsible for the injury— maybe even the death—of Biff Hooper? Joe knew he couldn't live with himself until he found Biff— healthy and in one piece.

Sheriff Kraft pulled up to the outer perimeter of the Ultimo Survival Camp. Ahead was a mesh fence topped with heavy, rusted barbed wire. At a small guardhouse, a young man in camouflage fatigues stopped and asked for identification, and then waved them through.

"Was that a rifle on that young man's shoulder?" asked Mrs. Hooper.

Nobody answered. The M-16 on the kid's back was answer enough.

They drove past areas where instructors were drilling groups of teens in vigorous calisthenics. Beyond them, where gray stone cliffs thrust up, an instructor was demonstrating rappelling techniques.

Joe's attention was caught by a squat blockhouse half-hidden by a stand of maple trees. It looked like a military command center, built out of cinder blocks, with bars on the windows, a satellite dish in the yard, and an antenna poking out of the roof.

As the sheriff's car pulled up to the front of this building, a man stepped from the doorway.

"We've had no problems before this with the Ultimo Survival Camp," Sheriff Kraft said gently to Mr. Hooper. "But they do rough it out here, make no mistake about that. Do away with all the modern conveniences. Part of their appeal, I guess.

"Today, I couldn't personally get hold of Orville Brand, the guy who runs this place. There aren't any phones on the premises, and as you can see, they're pretty isolated out here. I sent my deputy ahead to tell them we were coming, though."

Let's get on with it, Joe thought. He opened the back door and stepped out. Frank watched him, then glanced at Mr. Hooper.

As Joe walked around the back of the car,

Sheriff Kraft opened his door. The man who had emerged from the building stopped near him.

"Sheriff Kraft."

"That it is. Good to see you, Major Brand." Sheriff Kraft extended his hand, and the two men shook.

"And you, too," Brand answered with a slight smile. His hair was shaved to the scalp, which appeared white in contrast to his sun-weathered face. His skin seemed to be too tight over his face, a thin layer covering muscle and bone, so lean that it was almost skeletal. He had hard, high cheekbones and dark, deep-set eyes.

He walked briskly around the front of the car and opened the door for Mrs. Hooper before she could do it herself. He even bowed slightly.

"I'm sorry to hear of your trouble, Mrs. Hooper." Brand's voice sounded better suited to barking orders than to soothing people. "Whenever one of the boys in my outfit went missing—"

Joe stalked up to Brand and stopped in front of him, the door between them. "Thanks for your concern, but just tell us what's going on, will you?"

Brand was silent for a moment, staring at Joe. The skin over his face seemed to stretch almost to the breaking point. Large teeth showed behind his pencil-thin lips.

"I'll forgive your bad manners," Brand said.

He reached a hand into the car to help Mrs. Hooper out. "I am saddened to hear about your son. But, as I telegrammed, I checked our records thoroughly, and I even had the entire camp searched."

His dark eyes were unreadable as he paused to consider his next words.

"But nobody here," he announced, like a juror delivering a death sentence, "has ever seen or heard of anyone named Biff Hooper."

Chapter

3

THE EXTERIOR OF the Ultimo Survival Camp command center might look like a wartime bunker, but inside it was a startlingly modern office.

Fluorescent lighting made the big room shadowless. Against one wall stood a series of computers, their screens glowing with green letters.

The workers at the consoles, desks, and filing cabinets wore the same green fatigues as Brand. They worked as silently and efficiently as robots. Slit windows looked out on wide lawns and clusters of maple trees. Beyond these rose rugged, thickly wooded mountains.

Brand moved like an officer among his troops. He led Frank, Joe, Mr. and Mrs. Hooper, and Sheriff Kraft to one of the console operators. "Marsha, could you key in our roster file for these good people?"

The young woman nodded, her reddish blond hair in striking contrast to her green fatigues.

Frank, who was quite adept at operating a computer keyboard, admired the woman's expertise as her fingers moved briskly over the keys.

Letters appeared on the screen. Mrs. Hooper leaned forward anxiously, her pale face acquiring an eerie green glow. Her husband stood behind her, his face pinched and white.

The access code into Ultimo's computer roster system flashed onto the screen. The code letters read: GRUNTS.

"Cute," Frank whispered to Joe. "It's slang for soldiers," he told the Hoopers. He wondered if the entrance code was Brand's idea of a joke. He didn't seem the humorous type.

Marsha quietly punched other keys, and page after page of personnel and attendee rosters flashed on the screen. They all leaned toward the screen, watching anxiously for Biff's name. It did not appear.

"These rosters go to all squadron section leaders every morning, so they know exactly who is in their groups that day. The rosters come directly from this entrance computer list. I hand deliver them, first thing after breakfast." Brand's thin lips barely moved as he spoke.

Joe meandered away from the screen and the drone of Brand's voice.

Okay, he told himself, it's a foregone conclusion. We aren't going to see Biff's name on that list. So, what exactly does that mean? That Biff was never here? Or that his name has been eliminated from the computer memory?

He could still hear Brand speaking over the quiet click of the computer keyboards. He stopped before a bank of filing cabinets on the opposite side of the room. Above them was a large photograph framed in ornate, carved wood. Funny, he thought, an old-fashioned frame in this ultrasophisticated office.

In the picture were two soldiers in combat fatigues, both carrying weapons, both with grease-smeared faces. Commandos, Joe realized. One of the men was Brand. The other was— unbelievable. His huge, muscular body dwarfed Brand. Even his hands and fingers appeared too thick, making the pistol he carried seem like a child's toy. Joe looked more carefully. That "toy gun" was a Super Blackhawk pistol. Its barrel was seven and a half inches long.

The man wore a bandanna knotted about his forehead, but it was hardly to hold back his hair, which was cut as short as Brand's.

What stood out most clearly was a tattoo of a snake twisting about a human victim on the man's rippling biceps. The body of the snake traveled down the arm. The head, etched upon the biceps, had its fangs sunk into its helpless captive.

Brand had noticed Joe's departure and walked across the room toward him.

Joe crooked a thumb up at the photograph.

"Who's this guy? He looks like a real gorilla."

"That is our camp founder," Brand answered. "I served under him in 'Nam. He saved my life."

He leaned toward Joe, and something seemed to spark deep in his dark eyes, just for an instant. "If it weren't for him, I'd have been left for dead out in the jungle. I had three bullets in me. He stopped my bleeding and carried me to the medics—seven hard miles. He felt every step of it. I was unconscious, but others told me what he'd done, how he'd saved me." The spark in the dark eyes died.

"Hey, I didn't mean any disrespect," Joe said. Maybe he'd simply gotten a bad first impression of Brand. Yet, as helpful as Brand appeared to be, there was something about him that was just *wrong*.

A smile stretched Brand's thin lips. He clapped Joe's shoulder heartily.

"So, Joseph, if I were you, I would be careful about making light of the colonel. He is much revered and loved. A lot of people here might take—offense at any offhanded or untoward comments about him."

Brand turned to the rest of the group. "Speaking of my staff, you'll have the chance to observe them—and how they put the colonel's philosophy to work—as you tour our facilities."

"Wait a minute, Major Brand," Mr. Hooper said, his voice sharp. "We don't want a tour of this infernal camp. We want our son. We think you accepted a minor here for training without getting parental consent. Now he's disappeared, and it's your responsibility to help us find him."

"I told you," Brand said testily, "your son has never been here. He doesn't show up on our computer records, and our records are never wrong."

"Well, then, where is he?" countered Mr. Hooper. "He told his friend Joe here that he was coming to your camp. Biff doesn't lie."

Major Brand met Mr. Hooper's gaze calmly. "Obviously, he never got here. Maybe he stopped on the way. Maybe he changed his mind and never came to Georgia at all."

And maybe, thought Joe, there's something you're trying to cover up.

"We're checking into those possibilities," the sheriff said soothingly.

"Since we're here, we might as well get the tour," Mrs. Hooper said wearily. "That way we can satisfy ourselves that Biff really isn't on the camp's grounds."

"That's better," Brand said smoothly. "I don't often give tours myself, so you're getting the red-carpet treatment. Now, if you'll wait here for a moment, I'll go get the necessary keys from my office."

He saluted the group and pivoted toward the door. Mrs. Hooper put her arm through her husband's, and they walked over to a window to look out.

"Charming guy," Frank said sarcastically.

"He's done something with Biff. I know it, and I'm going to get him," Joe said, pounding his fist in his palm.

"Cool it," Frank said. "Sure, he's a slimy creep who knows more than he's letting on. But a confrontation won't get you anywhere. We need a technological edge—like a trusty portable computer."

"Where can we get one out here?" Joe asked.

"Mine is waiting for us back in the hotel room," Frank replied, smiling devilishly.

Brand was like a top salesman or politician as he conducted the tour. He knew how to talk a lot, tell lots of little anecdotes, yet say absolutely nothing.

Brand led them in a vast circle around the office, which was at the center of the grounds. At the base of the mountains was a series of barracks, built up on wooden planks, with crawl spaces beneath them. Each building had a placard by the door, stenciled with the name of the counselor in charge.

They passed a number of teens eating their lunches from mess kits, talking about what they had learned that morning, or telling "war stories" of previous survival games. They were almost fanatically clean-cut and in top physical condition.

No one had heard of Biff Hooper. Nor did anyone have a single bad word to say about the camp. As Brand led the way toward the area where mountain climbing techniques were taught, Joe lagged behind.

He quickly picked out several of the camp counselors, all in pressed, tailored fatigues. He wanted to question them, away from Brand. He described Biff to several of the counselors, but no one had seen him.

Joe started back toward the group, hoping Brand hadn't seen him disappear. He followed them up an incline that led into a wooded area. Running through the trees, Joe spotted something to his left. He stopped for a second and stared.

Barbed wire.

Should he continue to try to catch up with the group? It would only mean a slight detour to check the wired area.

Joe ran quietly over to the wire fence. A large sign was attached to a fencepost, and he saw several other signs in either direction. The signs read: No Trespassing Allowed Beyond This Point. Restricted Area. DANGER.

Why isn't this on the guided tour? Joe wondered. Maybe it's something Brand doesn't want us to see. I think I'll take a look.

He took out his Swiss Army knife and snipped out two sections of wire. Even though he stepped through carefully, a twisted barb snagged his pants, leaving a small rip at the knee.

Joe set off through the trees at a fast clip. Got to get in and out as fast as possible, he thought.

He scanned the area, trying not to miss anything.

He had not gone far when the trees began to thin. He reached a wide, hilly area, overgrown with long golden grass. There were thickets, some trees, something else he couldn't quite figure out—about two dozen dirt mounds. Something must be hidden just beneath the surface, but what?

Joe calculated for a moment. Brand would have noticed his absence by now and would probably be looking for him. He'd be easily spotted if he stepped into the open to check out those mounds.

Shrugging, he dashed out, stooped over and using available bushes for cover, he reached one of the mounds and started scooping away the dirt and sand. What was buried under the surface?

He had just hit something hard when the ground beside him erupted, spraying dirt into his eyes. Joe fell back, half-blinded, as something burst from the ground. "What the—?" he said.

He was facing a life-size wooden cutout of a man carrying a gun. The figure, which was masked, had just been thrust up from the mound.

Then a shot thundered through the air, and a bullet ripped through the painted chest of the wooden man looming over Joe. It tore a jagged hole in the figure and sent a shard of wood flying that hit Joe in the face.

Sand and dirt were spraying up everywhere as more and more guns joined in the firing. Mound after mound erupted with pop-up soldiers like a cardboard army of villainous jack-in-the-boxes. The roar of gunfire was continuous now. Bullets ricocheted off nearby rocks as Joe squirmed backward.

Too late, he realized where he was.

He was trapped in the middle of a target range—and he was the target!

Chapter

4

JOE HARDY SWEPT the back of his hand across his stinging cheek. A thin smear of dirt and blood rubbed onto his hand. He was already moving, rolling toward the nearest scrub grass-covered hill. Got to get out of here. Grab some cover, he kept repeating to himself.

A new wave of gunshots smashed into the wooden figures. Bullets ripped through the dirt around him, even though he was clear of the clustered targets.

He kept rolling, his world shrunk to that little hillock. A near miss sent sand spraying into his eyes. The noise was deafening. Keep moving! he urged himself.

Joe heard shouting. It seemed very faint, under the staccato of gunfire. But he thought he recognized the voice—Brand's.

"Cease fire! Cease fire!" Brand yelled, charging from the tour group toward the firing line. *"Live target on range!"*

Only a few steps behind Brand, Frank Hardy raced toward the hill. They had reached the line of trainees now. The instructors had taken up the call of "Cease fire!"

But Frank still heard shots. He knocked a rifle from one kid's hands.

"Are you deaf?" he shouted furiously. "Can't you hear? You want to get somebody killed?"

"Killed? What?" the kid asked, looking down at the gun in confusion.

Brand strode off across the field. He shouted back to the counselors, "Secure all weapons from the trainees immediately. Make sure all weapons are unloaded."

The counselors quickly followed his orders.

"Sheriff, if you would kindly follow me!" Brand called without looking back.

Frank didn't wait for an invitation. He followed in Sheriff Kraft's footsteps.

Joe Hardy had continued to roll during Brand's cease-fire orders. That little hill has got to be near, he had thought, astonished that he hadn't been hit yet by a bullet.

Then he realized that something had changed. The thunder had stopped.

Joe was behind the tiny hill, flat on his back.

He lay gasping as if he had run a marathon, blinking his sand-filled eyes.

His vision slowly came back. The first thing he saw was a pair of combat boots striding toward him. Brand, Joe thought, shaking his head, trying to free his eyes of grit. I must be seeing things.

But Brand was still there, towering over him. Joe stared up into dark eyes raging with fury. Brand's leathery fingers were curled into fists, ready to strike. But then the major glanced over the hill and forced himself to relax.

He wanted to hit me. But not in front of witnesses! Joe thought.

Frank and Sheriff Kraft rounded the hill.

Brand spoke in a harsh, grating whisper. "Do you know you might have been killed?"

Shakily, Joe got to his feet. If he had to have it out with this man, he'd do it standing up.

"Sure, I figured that out right when I found out this wasn't the camp softball field. I didn't realize—"

"Didn't realize?" Brand fumed. He looked at Sheriff Kraft. "I swear to you, Sheriff, we have never had an accident like this in the entire history of our camp. This area is cordoned off with barbed wire and is clearly marked as restricted—no trespassing allowed!" Brand looked back at Joe accusingly. "But, then again, we usually have only mature young men here, not lunatics!"

Joe was mute.

"Say it!" Brand demanded. "Tell the sheriff. Admit that you saw the warning signs."

"I did," Joe said quietly.

"Then you purposely chose to disregard them. It isn't easy to get through that fence. You had to work at it to get yourself into such a dangerous situation. What could have possessed you?" Brand growled.

Joe glared at him in frustration. *I could say that I was looking for Biff, but that would sound phony. Especially since Brand just saved my tail.*

A counselor appeared beside Brand, removing his cap. He had wispy hair and on the right side of his scalp, a curved bald spot in the shape of a sickle. It was a scar from a very old wound—hair didn't grow over scar tissue.

"All the weapons have been emptied and locked up, sir," he reported.

"Thank you, Sergeant Collins," Brand said succinctly.

As Collins did an about-face in the sand and started to return to the firing line, Joe caught a glimpse of something attached to his utility belt. It hung from a strap and slapped against his thigh as he walked—a pair of goggles.

Dark rubber goggles with oddly shaped lenses.

Octagonal? Was that a suggestion of silver on the dark rubber?

Brand stepped in front of Joe, cutting off his sight line. "Come along."

Joe moved to try to get another look at Collins, but by then the counselor was too far in the distance. I want another look at those goggles, he thought. He remembered the aftermath of that wild survival game, how Biff had slapped his thigh with his night-vision lenses, how the silver initials had glinted.

Brand led them back toward the area where Mr. and Mrs. Hooper were still standing. He and the Sheriff were far enough ahead of the Hardys so that Joe could quickly tell Frank about the glasses on Collin's belt.

"I wanted to demand to see them," Joe said. "But how could I? Brand's already got everyone convinced that I'm a dangerous hothead."

"You gave him some help on that," Frank said, "blundering onto the target range."

In fact, Brand was already pouring it on as they arrived. "Fortunately, most of our charges here understand the dangerous nature of weapons," Brand was saying. "They know that rifles are not toys. And they follow the strict rules that are laid down for their own safety."

As they reached Mr. and Mrs. Hooper, Brand turned to Joe and attempted a smile. "I'm sorry if I was harsh with you," he said reasonably. "But you must understand that that was a foolish thing you did."

"It's a mistake I won't make again," Joe promised.

"Ah! I'm glad!" Brand said. He was really smiling now.

"We've taken up enough of your time," Sheriff Kraft said. "Thanks for being so understanding. You can see how concerned the Hoopers are."

"Certainly, Sheriff," Brand answered. "I only wish I could do more. Come, let me escort you back to the car." Brand walked off the firing line.

Mrs. Hooper stopped and looked up at Joe, her eyes bleak.

"Biff's not here." Her voice was hoarse. "I wish you hadn't been so certain we'd find him." Then she walked away blindly.

Frank and Joe both stared at her back, wishing there was something they could say.

"We'll find Biff," Frank called after her. "Whatever it takes."

"Very admirable."

Brand's voice startled the Hardys. They had not been aware that he had returned.

"I like a man who doesn't desert his friends," Brand said as Frank and Joe followed him down the slope in the direction of the command center.

They passed the blockhouse, then walked in silence to the police car. Before Joe climbed into the backseat, he stopped and looked back at Brand. He knew it wouldn't be the last time he'd tangle with that guy.

If those were Biff's goggles, Joe told himself,

then Brand knows Biff was here. And if Biff is or was here and then disappeared—well, then it looks like this place isn't all fun and games!

"That was a real interesting tour," Sheriff Kraft said. "Much obliged."

"Feel free to drop by again," said Brand as one professional to another.

"Hey, maybe you'll see me again, too," Joe said blandly.

"I'll look forward to it," Brand replied.

Both meant more than they were saying. Under their words was a promise—and a threat.

For a long moment, Joe met Brand's hard, cold stare. So this guy teaches people how to survive, he thought. The only question is, how well did Biff learn his lessons?

Chapter
5

"I'M NOT ARGUING with you, Joe," Frank Hardy said, sitting on one of the beds in their hotel room. He did not look up at his brother, who was pacing furiously. Instead, he tapped the Access key on his lap computer.

"Well, then, you're not agreeing enough," Joe countered, stopping at the one window in the room.

It was only nine-thirty that night, but the whole town of Clayton had shut down. There were neither cars on the street nor people on the sidewalks. Joe noticed a black van parked just beyond the glow of light thrown by the nearest street lamp.

Frank tapped GRUNTS and then, ACCESS TO ROSTER FILE on the keyboard. "I know you feel responsible for Biff's disappearance." He was speaking almost absently as he worked on the computer. A grim smiled appeared on his face as the first roster sheet of the Ultimo Survival Course appeared.

"I guess I am acting a little crazy over it." Joe turned away from the window, leaning against the frame. "Mrs. Hooper kept laying a guilt trip on me, all the way back to the airport." He sighed. "Then, as she was boarding the plane, she asked me to forgive her. Said she was so worried about Biff that she didn't know what she was saying."

"And?" Frank asked, continuing to type. He started noting down the home phone numbers beside each trainee's name.

Joe slammed a fist into his open palm. "It just made me feel worse! I don't know what's going on here, but I'm not leaving until we've found Biff! If he didn't want to go to the Ultimo Survival Camp, why did he make such a big deal out of telling me?" He whirled toward Frank. "I tell you, Brand is covering up Biff's disappearance!"

Frank looked up from the computer. "Okay. Nice theory. The only problem is, why? What reason could the camp have for kidnapping Biff? We've seen for ourselves that they're a legitimate business with a high safety record. Sheriff Kraft vouched for that, even though he admitted he wasn't thrilled to have a place like it operating in his jurisdiction."

Frank disconnected the computer from the phone between their two beds and began dialing a number.

"Who are you calling?" Joe asked. "I don't think they have takeout pizza service around here after the sun goes down."

Frank kept dialing, but he looked at Joe and grinned. "While you were busy getting Major Brand good and riled, I learned how to break into the camp's computer system."

He put the phone to his ear, listened to ringing on the other end. "Now, I thought we'd talk with these supposedly satisfied customers. You know, check if any other parents had kids who never returned. Let's see if they really do give a product endorsement."

Joe jumped up in the air, making a victory gesture with his fist. "Frank! You're a genius!"

After the first three calls, Joe stopped listening. He slumped on the bed. None of the attendees had disappeared. They vouched for the camp like actors in a television commercial.

Joe thrust himself off the bed, stalking back to the window. The street was still quiet. The black van was still parked just beyond the circle of light.

Frank hung up the phone with a clatter. "Well, that idea's a bust."

Joe spun around from the window, excitement lighting his blue eyes. "Wait a minute! Wait a minute!"

"Uh-oh," said Frank. "The great brain is at work."

Joe ignored the crack. "Sheriff Kraft told us about the investigation he did. But I just thought of something he *didn't* do."

Frank turned off his computer. "Such as?"

"The police checked flights into the airport to see if anyone had noted Biff's arrival."

"Right. Sheriff Kraft told us that," Frank admitted with a shrug. "So what?"

"So, Biff didn't have a lot of money. What if he came in by another route? Suppose he came in by bus?" Joe grabbed Frank's arm and yanked him off the bed. "Come on! I know you'll want to see the nighttime hustle and bustle of the Clayton, Georgia, bus terminal."

Joe approached a ticket window and started to describe Biff. Almost before he began, the clerk interrupted him.

"Sure, sure," he said, sounding grateful for anything that might enliven the humid night. There were only a handful of people in the terminal, and most of them were sleeping on benches. "I saw that boy, right here."

"You did!" Frank exclaimed incredulously.

"Yeah! Except I didn't see him arriving. Saw him leave about a half hour ago."

Joe scarcely dared to breathe. "Half an hour ago!"

"Sure enough. He bought a ticket for Fayette-ville."

Frank looked at Joe, puzzled. "Why would Biff want to go to Fayetteville?"

"You got me," the ticket clerk said, shrugging. "But customers don't have to tell why they're going where they're going. Long as they pay the fare, they can go any doggone place they want."

"Come on." Joe grabbed his brother's arm. "We'll find out when we've caught up with him."

It took them another hour to catch up with the Fayetteville bus.

Frank was at the wheel of the rental car, a worn sedan with sloppy alignment and virtually no pickup. "This crate was not built for speed," he said as they jarred against a rut. "Especially on a road like this."

The bus did *not* go on the interstates. Instead, it took dark, back country roads that twisted maddeningly through the hills and pine forests.

It was not a route to drive blind. But that was what Frank was doing, sometimes going into wild tire-screaming skids as they navigated lethal hair-pin turns in the middle of nowhere.

"How about staying on the road?" Joe asked, unable to resist needling his brother.

"Why don't you—" Frank stopped and con-centrated on avoiding a tree. "This stupid wheel keeps pulling to the right." He breathed a sigh of relief when their high beams finally picked up the rear of the bus.

Joe stared intently through the bug-splattered windshield of the car.

"Pull up alongside. Maybe we can get a glimpse of him"

"Lots of luck," Frank muttered, shaking his head.

"Just do it, will you? How else can I see if Biff is in there?"

Frank swung the car to the left and stepped on the gas. The road veered, but at least there were no lights coming toward them. The rental car inched up beside the bus.

One of the unwashed, center windows of the bus was lit. Someone was sitting up, head tilted down, obviously reading.

Joe rolled down his window, as if that could help him see through the mud-smeared bus window.

Then he reached back and grabbed at Frank's arm. They hit a rut just then, and the car went swerving over toward the wheezing bus.

"Let go!" Frank yelled, getting the car back under control. "If you're going to start acting like a maniac, at least give me some warning."

But Joe was paying no attention to his brother. His eyes were locked on the bus window. "It's Biff!" he shouted, astounded. "It's got to be!"

Chapter

6

"MAKE THIS GUY pull over!" Joe urged, never taking his eyes from the bus window.

"Cut off a bus while going *down* a hill?" Frank stared at his brother for a second, then shrugged. "Sure, why not? We've been driving like maniacs all night."

They were nearing the outskirts of a small town—little more than a widening in the road. The buildings were all dark, clustered at the foot of the hillside.

But Joe's attention was focused on that half-visible face in the bus. Come on, pal, turn toward me, he thought. He could see unruly blond hair, but the features were blurred by the film of dried crud on the glass. The head was still bent.

"Biff's probably checking up on the latest survival tactics," Joe said. "And he'll need them.

41

I'm going to hit him over the head for all the grief he's given us."

Frank leaned on the horn as he speeded up to pass the bus. The driver didn't give Frank an inch, staying right in the middle of the road. The rental car's wheels whined on the gravel shoulder.

With a quick twist of the wheel, Frank swung the car in front of the bus. Then he began slowing down. In his rearview mirror, he could see the bus driver glaring in disbelief as he hit his brakes.

The bus groaned to a stop. Joe leapt out of the car before Frank had completely stopped and raced up the hill to the bus. Its doors remained firmly shut.

Joe hammered on the glass. "Please, open up! It's an emergency!"

The bus driver merely stared down at him, scowling.

Frank joined Joe at the bus door. "Sir, we're assisting the police in searching for a missing person who may be aboard this bus. I'm Frank Hardy and this is my brother, Joe. We're detectives."

The driver pulled on the lever that swung the door wide. "Detectives!" He gave them a long, suspicious look. "You two look like a pair of punks to me. Now beat it."

Joe ignored the bus driver's command, leaping up the steps. He ran past the driver and down the dimly lit aisle.

Most of the seats were dark, except for the one halfway down. There, the ceiling light cut through the gloom onto blond hair and the face below it.

Joe halted. He felt as if someone had slugged him in the stomach. The air left him in a rush.

That face did not belong to Biff Hooper!

"You're not—" Joe began.

The man bounced up from his seat and launched himself forcefully into Joe. He was built like a fullback on steroids. The impact knocked Joe into a seat where a huge woman sat with a Siamese cat in her lap. Both the woman and the cat were asleep, and both awoke screaming and flailing when Joe hit them. Hands and claws raked at him.

"Help! Help! Help!" The lady's sentiments were echoed by the cat in the same high pitch.

Frank was standing near the bus driver, explaining the situation, when he heard the bedlam. He looked along the interior of the bus, wondering what was going on. Then he saw a massive, blond-haired figure charging at him.

Frank started to bring his arms up, trying to decide if there was anything he could say that would calm the man.

He had no chance. The figure bent low and dove at him, the blond head smashing into his stomach. Frank was hurtled into the bus driver's lap and sprawled out across the wheel. The bus horn began blasting.

The blond man jumped off the bus and tore off down the hill.

Joe freed himself from the woman and her cat. The woman had calmed down, but the cat was still clawing and screeching wildly as Joe dashed up the aisle.

The bus horn had stuck when Frank fell against it. Passengers were awakening. Everyone was shouting questions. Frank shoved himself off the bus driver, who was attempting, without success, to shut off the infernal racket of the horn.

Joe reached Frank, but didn't stop. He leapt off the bus and kept on running. Frank was right behind him. "What did you say to get that guy so upset?" Frank asked breathlessly.

"Didn't say a word. But he knew who I was. I'll swear to it."

They ran past their rental car. Ahead of them, at the bottom of the hill, the man ducked down a side road, taking a quick look back to see if they were following.

They reached the side road at the same time and continued running.

"You see him?" Joe asked, panting.

"Yeah. Going over that hurricane fence at the end of the road. Looks like the other side is some kind of store parking lot!"

They ran past houses with broken-down wooden fences. In the street old, rusted hulks of cars stood on tireless rims. The scent of oil was in the hot night air. Junk-food wrappers littered the grass and sidewalks, and most of the houses were unpainted. Frank suddenly felt very far from Bayport.

They scrambled over the hurricane fence as the man reached the shadowy rear wall of the store. There were other stores near it, all dark, all obviously closed, some permanently boarded over.

There was the sound of breaking glass. "He must have used his elbow to smash in a back window," Joe said. "I think he just climbed into the store."

Frank and Joe reached the broken window less than a minute later. They hugged the wall of either side of the window frame. Both were breathing heavily. The interior of the darkened store was ominously quiet.

"He could be waiting for us," Frank whispered.

"There are two of us," Joe said in a loud voice, then without hesitating he went in through the broken window.

As Frank climbed in after him, Joe was looking at the shadowy counters which formed narrow aisles.

A sporting goods store: basketballs, weights, little golf gizmos, a rack of baseball bats.

Joe stopped beside the bats, hefted one in his hand.

The blond guy stepped out at the end of the aisle just as Frank joined Joe.

"Glad you could make it," he said with an

arrogant grin. "Though it would have been better for my team if you could have waited until we made the stop in town. They're going to be annoyed, missing out on your elimination. It's too bad, but some players just don't make it through the game."

Frank and Joe started cautiously down the aisle. Joe let the bat dangle from one hand.

"All right. Stop right there!" The man held up his hand. He held a grenade in it. "I bet you know what this baby can do. So no cute tricks."

"How'd you know we'd be checking the bus terminal?" Frank asked as he came to an abrupt stop.

"We checked you out at the airport. As soon as we learned you hadn't left town, we kept you under surveillance."

"The black van just beyond the street lamp?" Joe asked.

"You got it. We had a shotgun microphone aimed at your window and heard everything you said. So when you went to the terminal, we were all set. I was the decoy to lure you out of town."

The man reached up and pulled off his blond hair. It was a wig. "Now we've got you alone, and we can take care of you. All I have to do is make a phone call—" He broke off in midsentence and hefted the grenade. "You have no objections, right?"

As the man spoke, Frank and Joe glanced meaningfully at each other. They didn't need any further communication. They began to inch apart, in order to offer separate targets.

When the man realized what they were up to, he threw the blond wig down violently, pulled the pin on the grenade, and raised his arm, ready to throw it.

"Stop that!" he yelled.

It was as if he had shouted a signal. The Hardys dove wide in opposite directions. But they didn't get far in the crowded store. Frank crashed into a shelf full of catchers' mitts. Joe knocked over a rack of fishing poles.

"All right, wise guys, this will still get one of you." The man hurled the grenade directly at Joe.

Pushing himself up from the tangle of fishing poles, Joe saw the deadly green sphere tumbling toward him. It wasn't going to miss!

Chapter

7

JOE FOUND IT difficult to really believe that something as small as a grenade could be so destructive. Yet, within seconds of the release of the pin, that little olive green ball would explode into a bundle of shrapnel, capable of digging an inch deep into walls.

He watched it come toward him. The man had thrown it in a straight line, no fancy high curve, just hard and fast, right down the center. If it hit him and then detonated, he would be dead.

Joe raised the bat in his hands. It was almost an instinctive act, born of years of playing ball back in Bayport with Frank, Biff, Tony, and the other guys. Biff often threw just such a straight hardball.

Joe had no room to swing, confined by the counters. Instead, he bunted.

49

There was a dull whack of metal on wood. Then, *clack! clack! clack!* with a monotonous tap on the linoleum each time the grenade bounced back in the direction of the man who had thrown it.

The man's hard face lost all its arrogance. It went slack with shock, and his eyes widened. He spun about and frantically started to run away.

The grenade bounced, *clack!,* and wobbled off to the left, away from the man, veering toward a glass-enclosed counter, bouncing, bouncing, bouncing.

Then two feet from the counter, it exploded!

Heat and smoke erupted. Both Hardys hit the floor, hands over their ears. The blast was thunderous in the confined space. They didn't even hear the ceiling fall in.

Frank lay in the midst of the baseball glove display. Baseball players' signatures danced before his eyes. He was positive the explosion had rendered him deaf, until he heard Joe calling.

"Frank! Don't let him get away!"

Joe ran into the smoke. Frank shoved his way clear and staggered to his feet. He tapped his ear with the palm of his hand, trying to clear his head. He looked up for an instant, and did a double take. He could see stars.

The blast had ripped a huge hole out of a section of roof, and now gray smoke billowed through it in a rush.

Frank had taken half a dozen steps into the

smoke when he ran right into his brother. Joe was standing still.

"What's the matter?" Frank asked, trying to take small breaths so that he wouldn't inhale the smoke too deeply. "I thought you didn't want him to get away."

"He won't," Joe said in a somber voice.

Joe pointed. Frank looked through the smoke. Debris from the collapsed roof littered the floor in a huge pile. A human hand was thrust up through the wreckage. The fingers did not move. The grenade's metal pin was still wrapped around the man's forefinger.

"The authorities will be here pretty quick," Joe said, stumbling away. "We'd better put in a call to Sheriff Kraft. We may need him to verify who we are."

They found their way out into the night as the first sirens sounded.

The fire was an orange-and-gold inferno seen through a billowing haze. The firefighters' sooty faces looked grotesque in the light from the burning building. Shafts of water raised great arcs of gray smoke.

Frank and Joe were sitting alone in Sheriff Kraft's squad car. The store owner had arrived ten minutes before and kept repeating, "Grenades, grenades; we don't stock grenades," to anyone who would stop to listen.

Sheriff Kraft approached his car wearily. His

hat was tilted back on his head, and he had bags under his eyes. He didn't speak at first but leaned in and picked up a thermos and some cardboard cups.

"If you're anything like me, you could stand a cup of coffee," he said, sounding exhausted.

Joe nodded numbly.

"Most people don't almost get themselves killed twice in one day." Sheriff Kraft poured some coffee into one of the cups and handed it to Joe.

Joe blew softly on the steaming coffee. "I see they brought the body out."

Sheriff Kraft handed Frank a cup. "I know it makes you feel bad, son. But it wasn't your fault. That man was playing with death, carrying that grenade. You couldn't have known it would blow up the stored ammunition in the hunting sales area."

"Is that what it did?" Joe asked.

Sheriff Kraft sipped his own coffee. "You didn't know?"

"We couldn't see much after it went off," Frank said. "Joe stumbled on the body."

"Well, there's no identification on the man. Bus driver doesn't know who he was. In fact, he's still up the hill, trying to get that blamed horn unstuck. Sounds like a banshee!" Sheriff Kraft brushed a hand through his thinning hair.

He sipped his coffee, careful not to get any on

his short mustache or beard. The steam from the cup fogged his glasses.

"We've got two deputies patrolling the area, looking for the black van. Couple of folks saw it, but they said it took off when the store exploded. Looks like the whole town came out to see what happened."

Joe stared moodily into his cup of coffee. "Well, it's obvious that Brand set up that surveillance on us."

Sheriff Kraft wiped the edge of his sleeve across his glasses to clear them. "Mind telling me how you came to that conclusion?"

"Who else have we asked about Biff?" Joe argued. "I think Brand realized we weren't going to give up the search, so he had us bugged to learn what our plans were. And when he heard us discussing going to the bus station, he had his Biff impersonator head out there fast." Joe stopped suddenly. "I probably shouldn't have told you that."

Sheriff Kraft smiled grimly. "I see." He gave them a long look. "I think you boys watch too many movies and TV shows about southern sheriffs."

He took a sip of coffee and looked up at the smoke. "Well, being a lawman was what I always wanted to be. The sheriff's face grew serious. "I know you probably think I'm against you two meddling with this Ultimo Camp thing," he said.

"Maybe you even think I've got you labeled as troublemakers." He tossed the dregs of his coffee into the gutter and then looked from Frank to Joe.

"I'm here to tell you there's nothing further from the truth."

Joe glanced at Frank.

"I have a plan in mind," Joe said hesitantly, and climbed out of the car. Frank joined him.

"Well, now's not the time to keep it to yourself, Joe," said the sheriff. "I think we've decided we're on the same side. You know, I don't like having an armed camp right in the middle of my jurisdiction." He stared down at Joe.

"I want to find a way to get into that camp undercover," Joe said fiercely. "See what we can find out if our good buddy Orville Brand doesn't know we're around."

"Well, I don't rightly know how you'd go about doing that," Sheriff Kraft said, rubbing his chin. "But if you *did* figure out a way, and you *did* find some concrete evidence of wrongdoing, something I could take to a judge and get a search warrant for, I'd move right in."

"Just one problem—I haven't figured out how to get in," Joe said.

Sheriff Kraft said quietly, "Well, I hope you do, and I hope you find your friend."

Joe stared straight into Sheriff Kraft's eyes. "So do I. But—I'm not so sure anymore."

"What do you mean?" Sheriff Kraft questioned.

Smoke drifted past.

"If it was Brand who tried to kill us—well, I don't think he's trying to hide Biff anymore." Joe shuddered slightly. "He's trying too hard to stop *any* investigation. There's something bigger at work here—much bigger." He turned to Frank and said what had been on his mind all along. "Maybe their training got a little too rough—and Biff didn't make it!"

Chapter
8

FRANK AND JOE HARDY stood at attention in the early-morning mist, risking the threat of discovery. They both had on fake eyebrows and thin mustaches, and Joe sported a false gold front tooth.

It was just after six in the morning, and they were surrounded by Ultimo Survival Camp trainees. Sergeant Collins, the counselor with the sickle-shaped scar on his head, stood at the front of the group. He had a clipboard with a roster sheet attached in the crook of his right arm. He was taking roll call.

Collins had not yet shouted the names Fred and Jim Cassidy. Sheriff Kraft had suggested the names to Frank and Joe, and Joe hoped desperately that the names were on the sheet. If not, he and Frank would quickly be discovered and turned over to Brand.

57

"Atwood, E.," Collins read off the clipboard. The name echoed faintly.

"Here!"

It was the second morning after the explosion. Frank had figured out how to get them inside the camp compound without going through regular entrance procedures. They would never have slipped past Brand.

Using the Ultimo Survival Course's computer access code, Frank had broken into the camp's system and added the pair of fake names to Collins's squad. This tactic, he hoped, would allow them to bypass the command center—and Orville Brand.

"Bartlett, K.!" Collins called.

"Here, sir!"

In the middle of the night Sheriff Kraft had dropped them off in a wooded area on the edge of the Ultimo property. He had driven away before they began their efforts to sneak through the outer perimeter fences. No one could say he was a witness to illegal trespass.

"Brown, R.!"

"Right over here!"

" 'Here' or 'Present' will suffice," Collins said as a rebuke.

They had made their way through thick woods until they reached the base of the mountain. Just before dawn broke, they had hidden themselves in the crawl space under the barracks that housed Collins's troops. When reveille sounded and everyone clomped out of the barracks and down the steps to form a squad, Frank and Joe—now Fred and Jim—had stepped out nonchalantly from under the raised section and joined the ranks.

Now Collins was shouting names, but still he had not reached theirs. Joe wondered if Frank had truly managed to bypass the command center and gotten their names entered on the computer roster lists.

"Cassidy, F.!" Collins read.

"Here!" Frank called smartly.

Joe exulted. They had done it! Success!

They're trying to kill us, Frank thought, nearing the end of the morning's five-mile run. This had followed a set of a hundred chin-ups and endless sets of push-ups. The sun had not yet climbed above the mountains. There was still mist rising from the ground. And he was sweating. His lungs were laboring. His legs ached. No wonder they call this the Ultimo Survival Camp. It's a major accomplishment if you survive, he told himself.

Joe was relieved to get on the obstacle course. Ordinarily, climbing over fences and crawling through mud would not have been comforting. But at least he had managed to escape the mess hall, where they served the most disgusting scrambled eggs he had ever tasted.

If that hadn't been enough to make him lose his

appetite, Brand had strolled around the long breakfast tables. Both Joe and Frank had kept their heads bowed whenever he came anywhere near their table.

Collins had sat at the head of their table. He still had the pair of goggles at his waist that looked an awful lot like the ones Biff wore, but Joe would have to see the initials B.H. to be absolutely sure.

That was easier said than done. Collins treated his squad like a bunch of green recruits in boot camp; he kept his distance. Joe had seen rocks that were friendlier.

Now, as the squad approached the obstacle course, Joe drew abreast of Collins. "Uh, sir," he began.

Ignoring him, Collins spun about and ordered all the trainees to leave their personal belongings on a table nearby. Joe stared down at the goggles dangling at thigh level. Collins caught him.

"Something wrong with your ears?" he asked suspiciously. "And what are you staring at?"

"I was wondering where I could get a utility belt like the one you have," Joe replied.

"Let's just see if you can get through the course like a man," Collins snarled, "before you start thinking about dressing like one."

Joe positioned himself to begin the course. To his right, on a long table, were the trainees' personal belongings: watches, neck chains, hunting knives.

"Get going!" Collins ordered Joe.

Joe began the rigorous course. He hurdled fences, pulled himself across a rope strung over a huge, muddy pit, then crawled through a shallow ditch topped with barbed wire. But when he was at the top rung of a wooden barrier, he paused, looking back at the beginning.

Well, what do you know about that? Joe thought. Their drill instructor was going through the items left on the table. Collins was ripping off the trainees!

When he finished the course, Joe stretched out on the ground, exhausted. After about five minutes, one of the trainees ran up to Collins, an angry look on his face.

"My watch is missing!" the trainee complained.

Collins's right forefinger traced the livid white scar in his hair. "What's the matter, Bartlett? Can't keep track of your stuff? What do you think I am, your personal watchdog? You're responsible for keeping an eye on your own equipment, I just make sure you don't wreck it going through the course."

Collins gestured at the trainees who were recovering from the course. "Better check your buddies. One of them's not trustworthy."

Frank Hardy decided to skip the lunch of creamed chipped beef on soggy white bread.

He managed to find himself a good hiding place

in the maple trees that stood not far from the command center from which he could observe. There was a truck pulled up near the front door, and men and women in fatigues were carrying out record files and handing them up to others stationed in the back of the truck.

What were they doing? Packing up? Getting ready to abandon the camp?

It can't be! Frank told himself. He and Joe weren't on to anything yet that was of real danger to Brand's crew.

He heard a snap behind him. Someone was approaching through the trees nearby! Frank peered cautiously behind him. It was Brand, walking in his direction!

His mind raced. Should he sneak away? No. Any movement would catch Brand's eye. Frank would have to lie low. He tried not to think of what would happen to him if Brand tripped over him.

Brand did walk by, only six inches away.

Frank wished he'd gone in to eat the creamed chipped beef. But then he got a break. He could not hear Brand's words when the man stopped by the back of the truck, but he obviously ordered the people down and back into the center. Within moments the truck was clear.

Frank ran to the back of the truck, and went through the first batch of files he came to. He pulled one out at random and studied it.

The papers inside were mainly letters between

the Ultimo Survival Camp and Generalissimo Manuel Strosser, the merciless dictator of San Marcos. The papers outlined a business deal in which the camp would provide mercenary troops for the dictator.

Hardly able to believe what he had found, Frank continued to scan the page. But he came to an abrupt stop when he read the bottom line—the fee for those fully trained troops: one million dollars!

If Biff had discovered this, and if he'd been caught. . . . Frank couldn't stop the thought. It would certainly be a strong motive for getting rid of Biff—permanently!

Later that day Joe Hardy, a.k.a. Jim Cassidy, was in trouble! Collins saw it at once. He had been showing the greenhorns, as he liked to call them, how to climb up a mountainside. He had a headache and would rather not have been teaching wimps how to rappel. Only the dark-skinned one—what was his name, the kid over to his right, Fred Cassidy—had any talent for climbing and descent.

The brother, Jim Cassidy, was directly above Collins right then, only ten feet farther up the uneven rocky surface. Collins remembered how this blond kid had been staring at him just before the obstacle course. He could have sworn he had been watching him—as if he knew that Collins was about to check the contents of the trainees' table to see if they'd left him any little treats worth taking.

From where Collins hung from his rope, feet planted firmly against the side of the mountain, he could easily see the blond kid. Jim Cassidy had stopped on a narrow ridge covered with mountain laurel.

When Jim grabbed a handful of dark green branches in an attempt to gain some leverage, Collins knew there was trouble!

The roots pulled loose from the ledge. Specks of dirt splattered across Collins's face as Jim Cassidy's boots scraped against rock. His hands searched wildly for some kind of hold. He didn't find one. He fell backward, and now, like the dirt, he was hurtling downward!

Collins stared in disbelief as the kid's body grew rapidly larger.

He could only think one thought: This kid is going to get himself smashed to a pulp!

Chapter

9

JOE HAD NOT counted on Collins letting him fall.

The way Joe had it planned, Collins would reach out, like the seasoned mountaineer he was supposed to be, and snatch him from the long, bumpy descent to broken limbs or death! Collins, the hero of the day, with theft as a sideline. And then Joe could get a good look at those goggles dangling from Collins's waist.

The only problem was that Collins was *not* going to grab him. Collins had frozen in the clutch!

Joe scraped against the gray rock, hitting his thigh hard. That's going to leave one wicked bruise, he thought.

Joe twisted his body violently, one hand holding tight to the rope lashed about him.

Well, if Collins wouldn't reach out to grab him,

he would swing himself toward Collins and grab onto him!

He banged across the side of the mountain in a long swing that carried him down and to the left. He crashed right into Collins, who had thrust out his arms as if to stop him. As Joe's body slammed into Collins's stiffened fingers, the instructor's eyes went wide with pain. Joe wrapped his arms tightly around Collins's neck, as if he were afraid.

Don't put on the frightened pupil bit too thick, he silently warned himself.

The two of them swayed from Collins's anchored rope. Collins ripped Joe's arms from around his neck and shoved them up against the mountainside.

"Find a handhold there!" he shouted. "What are you trying to do, get us both killed?"

Collins pushed himself out from the cliff edge, holding onto his rope, and rappelled down from Joe a couple of feet. Joe could barely stop himself from screaming in anger. He still hadn't managed to get a clear look at the dark goggles.

"You take it nice and easy," Collins called to Joe, "and get yourself down to the bottom. And don't do any more stupid things like grabbing onto vegetation without having your rope secured."

Frank swung expertly over to Joe's side. Joe saw dread in Frank's brown eyes.

Oh, no, Joe thought. He really thought I was falling.

"You okay?" Frank asked tensely.

"Yeah. Sorry. I didn't mean to scare you," he whispered. "It didn't work out as I planned."

"You were almost killed twice in the last two days, and when I saw you falling, all I could think about was how people say things happen in threes." Frank also kept his voice to a whisper, but Joe could read his worry and anger.

"It was a spur-of-the-moment idea," Joe whispered.

"I hate your spur-of-the-moment ideas!" Frank hissed back.

Joe shrugged. "Sometimes I'm not too crazy about them myself."

Joe climbed cautiously down. Collins gave him a wide berth.

One of the trainees called over to Joe, "Hey, what happened up there? You slip on a banana peel?"

The other trainees, clinging like awkward spiders to the side of the cliff, laughed. Trainee Brown laughed so hard that his feet slipped and he was left dangling from his rope, which fortunately was secured. He stopped laughing.

As Joe passed by Collins on his way down he tried to get a clear view of the goggles, but they were hidden by Collins's leg. He could only see the tops of them. They were certainly similar to the ones Biff had had.

"Cassidy," Collins snapped. "The point of this camp is *survival*. You want to pull stunts, pull them at home—I shouldn't have to nursemaid you." He scowled. "Know what would have happened to me if you'd fallen?"

"I can't imagine," Joe answered, stopping his descent for a moment. "I was thinking about what would have happened to me."

"You'd have put me in bad with Major Brand," Collins said harshly. "I could have lost my job. He could have lost faith in me."

"Gee," Joe said as politely as he could, "I wouldn't want a thing like that to happen."

He could feel Collins glaring at him, all the way to the bottom of the mountain.

The next part of the plan was a little more complicated. Joe had to break into Collins's room and search for the goggles without getting caught.

Still, he decided, it had to be easier than Frank's job: making conversation with Collins.

It was dark in front of the rec hall. The trainees were inside, watching a double feature—*The Killer Commandos* and *Return of the Killer Commandos*. Except for Collins, who always ran the projector and claimed to have seen both films more than a hundred times, the instructors had taken off on their own.

"Hi," Frank said as he stepped in front of Collins.

Collins grunted, trying to move around Frank.

Machine-gun sound effects and explosions punctuated the night from the rec room.

"I just wanted to thank you for saving my brother's life out there," said Frank.

"Just my job, kid," Collins muttered and again tried to push past him.

But Frank was instantly in front of him again. "Look," he went on, "don't hold it against him, will you? Jim just hasn't done much rappelling. He—"

"Don't worry about it," Collins interrupted. He shoved Frank aside. "Now, do you mind getting out of my way?"

Inside Collins's dark room, Joe Hardy could hear Frank and Collins talking. His heart was pounding.

He surveyed the room, letting his eyes adjust to the dark. He didn't dare even turn on a flashlight. First he checked under the military cot in the center of the room. He could have bounced quarters off the tightly made bed.

Carefully, he slipped his hand under the mattress, making a wide, slow sweep to see if anything was hidden there.

Nothing.

Collins climbed the stairs that led to his room. Frank dashed up the steps and grabbed his arm. Collins whirled about and glared at him. "What is it now?" he asked.

Frank hesitated. What *was* he going to say now? "I—I was just wondering about tomorrow," he finally got out. "I thought maybe if you could tell me what's on the schedule, I could make sure my brother is better prepared."

Collins gave him a long, hard look. "Cassidy, I'll let you know what the schedule is when I let everybody else know. Now, either get back to the movie or go get some sleep. You'll need it." He turned and put his hand on the doorknob.

Joe was searching through the bureau drawers when he heard the footsteps on the stairs.

Not enough time! he thought.

Then in the next instant he heard the doorknob turning!

Frank firmly placed his hand on top of Collins's and pulled the man's hand off the doorknob. Collins turned to look at him as if Frank were crazy. In the moonlight, the scar on Collins's skull appeared very livid.

"Get your hands off me, you little creep," Collins snarled.

"I'm sorry," Frank said. "I just wanted to ask you a question."

"What question?" Collins asked, his eyes narrowing.

"I'm going rock climbing next month," Frank said in desperation. "In Washington State."

"That's lovely," Collins drawled. "Enjoy yourself."

Frank smiled again, the most pleasant smile he

could manage while making conversation with this glowering bozo. It made his face hurt.

"What I wanted to ask you," he pressed on, "is if you've ever played in the Cascades. I mean, do you have any tips about the area—things to watch out for, rope techniques . . ."

"Cassidy." Collins's voice hovered between boredom and outright irritation. "I don't think much of you *or* your brother. He's a pain in the behind, an awkward grunt. You're a little better—the best in the squad. You don't need my advice. So why are you trying to butter me up?"

Frank faked all the indignation he could dig up. "Butter you up? I thought I was talking one climber to another. I—"

Collins turned back to the door. "Kid," he said, beginning to turn the knob, "if you're not sucking up, I think you're crazy."

Joe finally found the hidden treasure in a shoebox tucked away on the top shelf of the closet. There were more wristwatches than an octopus could wear, all kinds of jewelry, different kinds of camping equipment—and a pair of octagonal goggles, with the initials B.H.!

I've got you, Collins! he thought. Then he heard the door start to open and knew he was going to be discovered.

"How about the Negev?" At this point Frank was willing to try anything.

Collins stopped. He stood with his back to Frank for such a long time that Frank was positive he wasn't going to reply. Then, Collins turned. Frank saw a really baffled look cross the sergeant's face.

"The Negev is in Israel," he said, trying hard to keep his patience.

"I know that," Frank said. "Haven't you ever done any desert climbing?"

"I did my desert training in the Sahara," Collins told him. "Lived for five days on one lousy canteen of water. Thought my skin was going to shrivel off in that sun."

Joe was climbing out the side window as Frank said, "What about the Himalayas? You ever done any climbing there?"

Frank and Joe were alone in the barracks, sitting on Frank's bunk, drinking Gatorade.

"Wow, 'Fred,' you made yourself look like a real jerk with Collins." Joe grinned. "But we've got him now—Collins and the whole camp."

The barracks stretched wide and long. Empty bunks stood in rows waiting for their occupants.

Joe took a swig of Gatorade. "If someone as sharp as Brand had anything to do with Biff's disappearance, you can bet he wouldn't leave any evidence around. I'll bet Brand doesn't even know Biff's goggles are around."

Frank gazed about the room. It seemed somehow ominous—too quiet, too empty.

"Okay," Joe said, "when the trainees come back in and lights go out, we wait a little while and then sneak out of here. We come back here with Sheriff Kraft and let him search Collins's room. When he finds Biff's goggles, he'll have good cause to turn this camp upside down."

Frank tilted the cup to his lips and drained his Gatorade.

"And the best thing is," Joe went on, raising his cup high, "we put it over on Brand. He doesn't suspect a thing."

Frank did not say anything. He was looking at his cup as if he were having difficulty focusing.

"What do you think, Frank?" Joe asked. "Will Brand be surprised when we come waltzing in here tomorrow or what?"

Frank let the cup drop out of his hand onto the mattress.

Joe yawned. "Hey, Frank? Why don't you say something?" He turned toward Frank and was surprised to see him half-lying on the bed, his feet still on the floor.

"What are you doing, falling asleep on me at a time like this?" Joe asked, standing.

Then he staggered. "What the—?" Joe grabbed for the bunk edge, missed. Frank's body on the bed seemed to blur. Drugged! The thought went through his mind. Only the lowest of the low would drug the Gatorade!

Joe tried to pull himself together. Anyhow,

how did Brand or his people even know we were here and drinking Gatorade?

As he slumped to the floor, Joe was aware that people were entering the room from the far end. Three, maybe four people at the most.

He could not make out their features. Flesh tones melted into cloth.

Someone knelt beside him. Was that a skeleton smiling?

No! The sunken eyes, burning darkly. He could make out the eyes—Brand's!

Brand's voice sounded very distant. "I told you I was looking forward to meeting you again."

They were the last words Joe heard. Then the world became lost in darkness.

Chapter

10

SOMETHING HURT!

Joe Hardy heard the harsh sound of flesh striking against flesh. Pain followed immediately. Slowly, he came to. Someone was slapping him across the face.

Again, Brand backhanded Joe, and the resulting surge of pain brought him fully back to awareness. Instinctively, Joe moved to defend himself, ready to hurl himself at Brand and take him out, no matter what the consequences. But his body jerked against a restraint at his waist. He couldn't move his hands.

Joe tried to comprehend why he couldn't strike out at Brand. He looked down at his wrists. They were strapped to the arms of a seat. He was belted across the stomach into a seat of plush maroon velvet.

He became aware of the drone of an engine as Brand straightened up. They were on a private plane.

"Stop hitting him!" he heard Frank say and realized that his brother was strapped into the seat beside him.

Brand gazed from Frank to Joe. The dark eyes held a flicker of joy—an eerie thing to see on that face.

"You both thought you were so clever," Brand said smugly, his narrow lips stretching in a cruel smile. "Well, you were, in a way. I try to give credit where credit is due." He shook his head. "Too bad about Collins. You were right, Joseph, I *was* surprised to find out about those goggles. Collins now has a matching scar on the other side of his head."

Frank tested the straps biting into his wrists. They didn't give an inch.

"On the other hand," Brand continued, "I always review the roster sheets when I hand them out. When I spotted both a 'Fred' and a 'Jim Cassidy' listed, specifically when I did not recall interviewing any trainees with the same last name, I knew it had to be you two. I figured I'd wait you out to see what your game was."

"Yes," Frank said bitterly. "We noticed you like to play games. With people's lives."

"You should feel honored." Brand walked over to the window and peered out at the clouds. "You are being taken to Colonel Hammerlock's private sanctuary." He turned back to stare at them. "To one of the best hunting grounds in the world."

Joe decided to goad Brand. It was a standard ploy he and Frank had agreed upon in case they were caught by an enemy: try to create a situation that might lead to a chance for escape. Keep the adversary talking—information could be a powerful weapon.

"Is that his real name, Hammerlock?" Joe asked sarcastically. "I know a wrestling coach who would love to have him on the Bayport High team."

Brand stalked impatiently past them in the center aisle of the plane. "Hammerlock is the code name he went under during the war. He was a hero then."

He leaned toward Joe, flashing his cadaverous smile. His hand whipped up, fast, before Joe could attempt to twist his head away from the blow. A vivid red mark colored Joe's face. "You shouldn't pick on people's names, Hardy," Brand went on calmly. "Especially when they aren't around. It's not polite. Do you want to make jokes about my name? Orville."

The smile disappeared, and the thin lips hardly seemed to move as he added, "When I was a teenager, my peers loved to make fun of my name. But not for long."

Frank glared directly into Brand's hate-filled eyes. "Personally," he said in a bright voice, "I love the name Orville. One of the Wright brothers was named Orville." He paused, making sure Brand was looking at him. "Too bad you dishonor the name."

Brand spun toward Frank, his hand raised. But before he could connect, Joe lifted his feet, tripping Brand. The major grunted in surprise and then, with the agility of a cat, regained his balance. He's not going to be an easy one to fight, thought Joe, noting the maneuver.

"How many missing teenagers are there besides Biff?" Joe asked, wanting to distract Brand before he went for Frank again.

Brand's right hand was clenched in a fist, and he was shaking with rage. Then, as Joe had seen on the target range, he uncurled his fingers, grew calmer and spoke with quiet tension. "A few dozen. An elite corps for the colonel."

"How'd you pull it off?" Frank asked in disbelief. "Dozens of kids disappear, and no one questions where they went?"

Brand chuckled. The sound seemed like bones scraping together deep in his throat.

"Do you know how many runaways there are in this country?" he asked, actually beginning to enjoy himself again. "No, I expect you don't. You two are nice and content in Bayport, though I suspect that friends of yours, like this Biff, perhaps are not as satisfied."

The plane started a descent. Out of the window Frank could see a stretch of ocean past the clouds.

"Some kids run to the cities," Brand continued. "Most of them are looking to get away from terrible home lives. But they find they ran to more terrible things than they ever imagined."

The plane was slanting down through the clouds now, piercing the vast cotton-candy sky.

"Some kids go looking for adventure—or a cause." Brand nodded. "That's what we offer to those who want it enough to pass the test."

"The games, you mean?" Joe guessed, wondering exactly where they were landing.

"The Ultimo Survival Camp was legitimate. It also provided a perfect recruiting system and raised generous funds for the colonel's real purposes. You two made a grave mistake when you forced us to abandon it." He ran a hand over his scalp. "You should have seen those trainees milling about as we took off from our private airstrip. They were quite beside themselves."

"I still don't understand how you and Colonel Hammerlock get away with it," Frank said, pretending admiration.

"You don't fool me with your transparent attempts to appeal to my ego," Brand snapped at him. "But there is no reason not to tell you. Where you're going is the last stop." He stared at the plane ceiling for a moment, as if considering what to tell them.

Joe rubbed his wrists against the strap. His flesh burned with the effort, but the strap remained taut as ever.

79

"It was all quite easy once we had the camp going. But you see, only a few applicants ever got to play the game for real. I personally selected the trainees who proved they would make superior warriors," Brand began.

Frank could see the tops of trees out the window and a stretch of lovely, deserted beach. They were approaching an island!

"Oh, no matter how good a trainee was, if he came to our course with his parents' permission—or if I found out that he had told lots of people where he was going—he was never even considered for indoctrination."

The green tops of trees rushed by directly under them.

"I talked with your friend Biff for several hours. He took me into his confidence while I was giving him personal instruction in combat." Brand shrugged. "I knew his parents didn't have the faintest idea where he had gone. And he was good at the game, a natural for combat. Perhaps I was a little eager."

The dark eyes turned to Joe, displeased. "Unfortunately, Biff did not tell me he had confided in *you*. I must admit, I was a little taken aback by first the inquiries and then your sudden visit."

The plane dipped. Joe's stomach lurched. The plane's wheels touched ground, bumping them about in their restraints.

"What's happened to Biff?" Frank asked, dreading the answer.

Brand shook his head sadly. "He hasn't been totally cooperative."

"Good old Biff!" Joe said with a laugh.

Those dark, reptilian eyes turned on Joe. "When you two showed up with the sheriff, well, you can imagine. I radioed the colonel—our people here had to interrogate the boy rather severely." Brand's voice made that sound as if it was a pity. "I'm rather afraid to see what, if anything, is left of him."

With that, Brand strode to the plane's cockpit. Moments later the Hardys were untied and escorted from the cabin at gunpoint.

Frank and Joe halted on the plane steps, stunned. Built into the side of a rust-colored mountain they saw a fantastic, old-fashioned fortress. High bastions stood at each corner of the stone edifice, and uniformed, armed guards patrolled the battlements. "It's authentic," Brand said proudly, "built in the eighteenth century to deal with pirates. With some renovations, it was quite suitable for the colonel's needs."

But Frank and Joe weren't noticing the scenery. Standing before the plane, directly ahead of them, was Colonel Hammerlock himself.

Brand shoved them forward. Both of the Hardys almost fell down the steps.

"Now, move!" Brand commanded.

Frank knew that Joe wanted to attack; his brother had been itching for action from the moment they'd been untied.

"Not now!" he whispered quickly. "Let's find out where Biff is and what kind of shape he's in first."

"Yeah. You're right," Joe muttered as they marched toward the colonel. In person, the colonel looked much as he had in his picture, but even larger and more impressive. He was bare-chested, except for a shoulder holster and a bandolier of ammunition. He stood in the hot sun, his powerful torso gleaming with sweat.

"Where do you think we are?" Joe whispered.

"Some deserted island in the Caribbean," Frank replied with a shrug.

Brand shoved Frank again. "Don't speak until you're spoken to," he ordered.

Colonel Hammerlock did not move until they reached him. He wore a red bandanna knotted about his head. He held a Super Blackhawk pistol trained on the Hardys. As he raised it level with Joe's eyes, a snake tattoo rippled along his arm muscles. The heavy gun seemed puny in his huge fist.

He surveyed Frank and Joe as if he could not believe what he saw. "You mean to tell me, Brand, that it was two no-accounts like this who forced us to close the center?"

Brand looked uneasy. "Sorry, sir. These are the ones."

Frank pointed to the gun. "That's not one of your trainee's target pistols," he observed.

"You're right," the colonel said in a guttural

voice. "This weapon fires eighteen rounds of MTM forty-four Magnum ammunition." Some of the colonel's words were slurred, and Joe realized that he suffered from partial paralysis on the right side of his face.

Colonel Hammerlock looked at the gun lovingly, then gazed at Frank. "The weapon has been tested on Asiatic water buffalo, as well as wild boar. Goes right through 'em. Imagine what it does to humans." With a laugh, the colonel turned and started toward the entrance to the fortress. Brand nudged the Hardys, and reluctantly they followed.

Inside, the colonel led them to a set of stone steps that descended into a network of subterranean corridors. The stone walls were damp. The air smelled of mud and decay.

"Where are you taking us?" Joe demanded.

"You'll see," Brand replied.

Finally they reached a cobblestone corridor that led past huge metal doors with small barred windows set at their tops. Water dripped somewhere in the deep shadows.

"We keep transgressors down here," the colonel informed them.

"Transgressors?" Frank asked.

"Recruits with capabilities that could have made them invaluable additions to our organization. Some foolishly decline our offer to serve, as if they think they really have an option. Others are simply too rebellious."

The colonel stopped at a door midway along the corridor and took keys from a belt about his waist. "Some are not willing to be, uh, team players."

"My kind of people!" Joe exclaimed defiantly.

The colonel unlocked the door. "Good!" he said, thrusting the door open. "Then you can enjoy dying alongside them!"

Brand shoved them through the doorway, and the steel door slammed shut with an ominous clang.

Frank and Joe stood still for a moment, waiting for their eyes to adjust to the darkness. The room they were locked in was a dirt-floored dungeon. Rats scampered near a battered, bloodied figure that lay very still, half-obscured in shadow.

"Oh, no," said Frank, darting forward. "Biff!"

Chapter

11

A LARGE RAT was sniffing around Biff's ankles.

Biff's hand feebly swiped at the rodent's well-fed body. Whipping its tail around, the animal let out a squeaky screech of protest, then fled into the shadowy recesses of the damp cell.

Frank felt a surge of adrenaline when he saw that weak gesture. It meant Biff was alive!

The Hardys knelt on either side of their friend. Gently, they propped him up against the stone wall.

Biff's face was swollen and bruised, but he managed a weak smile. "I knew you guys would find me. Knew it all the time."

"Yeah, we've got to get you back to Bayport. Football practice starts soon," Joe said, trying not to let Biff see how concerned he was. He knew he had to bolster Biff's hopes for escape.

Suddenly, Frank and Joe became aware of a

shuffling sound behind them. They turned to see two other prisoners who shared the same dungeon quarters.

"Frank?" Biff mumbled.

"Yeah?"

"This is turning out not to be fun." Biff sagged back against the wall.

Frank nodded solemnly. "The real thing seldom is." He stood and faced the two other prisoners. "Where are your manners, Biff? You haven't introduced us to your cellmates."

"Hi. I'm Terrence Scott. Just call me Terry," said a black teenager as he extended his hand in greeting. He was in much better shape than Biff.

Terry's hair was cropped close to his head. His brown eyes were almond shaped, and they glittered with an alert curiosity that even his surroundings couldn't lessen.

Terry was as tall as Joe, with a thin, wiry build. His handshake was firm.

"Hey, Terry," Frank said. "How did you wind up here?"

Terry shrugged. "Just lucky, I guess." He grinned. "Biff's talked a lot about you two. Your reputation precedes you."

He gestured awkwardly toward Biff's battered body. "We've tried to help Biff as much as we could. They worked him over pretty thoroughly a couple of days ago." Terry breathed harshly. "Not much we could do for him. They confiscated all our medical equipment."

"You were one of the game players at Ul-timo?" Joe asked.

"Yeah. Seemed like a good idea when I signed up. My father's an intelligence agent." Terry looked down at his muddied fatigues. "I thought I could follow in my dad's footsteps. Figured I'd impress him."

He took a deep breath. "Now I could kick myself for being so clever in covering my own tracks. I made it impossible for him to trace me."

In the silence, they could hear rat claws raking through dirt.

Terry turned to the remaining prisoner, who stood behind him.

"I suppose you'd like to meet the third occupant of our little abode." He held a palm out to indicate the figure, who stepped forward.

A girl! Joe thought, then corrected himself, a woman. She was about his age, seventeen. Did that make her a girl or a woman?

Her handshake was as firm as Terry's.

"I'm Lauren Madigan," she announced in a confident voice.

Her hair had been lightened by the sun to a golden blond. Her face was tanned, and her eyes were a clear blue. She stood just over five feet.

Lauren rubbed her hands together to keep them warm. "As long as we're telling life stories, I'll give you the condensed version of mine." She looked up at the high, hard ceiling, as if she could see her past up there. "I come from a large family

87

in the Midwest, five brothers and three sisters. The first time I ever played a survival game, it was like a revelation to me."

"What do you mean?" Joe asked.

Lauren kicked out at a rat that was creeping near her booted foot. "Oh, it's hard to explain. I guess it was the first time I felt like I'd achieved something on my own."

She stared after the squealing rat. "When you have so many people around you—brothers, sisters—you just feel like you're part of a group. That you've lost your own personal identity."

She looked directly at Joe. "Every time I played at survival, it gave me a feeling of independence. It was something none of my brothers or sisters could or would do. My parents didn't approve of the games. They thought the games were endorsing violence. I thought they were offering freedom." She surveyed the walls glumly. "And for a time, they were. But not anymore."

It was the weirdest dinner party Joe had ever attended.

In the early evening, Brand had visited their cell, inviting the five of them to dine with the colonel.

Not that there was a choice. Brand and several armed guards led them to a large room on the second floor of the fortress. Two guards supported Biff between them. Frank wondered how his friend would be able to sit through the meal.

Hammerlock's inner sanctum was a combination dining room and armory. The walls and floor were decorated with a vast array of weaponry: guns, crossbows, suits of armor, broadswords—a virtual history of weapons collected in one room.

The center of the room was dominated by a long, elegant table, surrounded by high-backed, hand-carved wooden chairs. A sumptuously woven tablecloth covered the entire length. Joe shook his head in amazement at the embroidered scene it depicted: medieval knights charged on horses; samurai warriors attacked with swords; Civil War soldiers battled with bayonets and cannons; and modern soldiers marched with M-16s. There were ornate candlesticks placed along the center of the table, each with a tapered, flickering candle. Seven filigreed metal plates were set out.

Colonel Hammerlock sat at the head of the table, and at his nod orderlies appeared and served dinner. I should have expected this, Joe thought as they placed army ration packages on top of the metal plates.

"Dig in!" the colonel ordered. He immediately ripped open his package, pulled out a can, and attacked the top with a small can opener.

"This tops everything," Terry muttered to Frank.

Joe found the can opener in his package, and

pulled out a green painted can labeled Peaches. He cut open the lid. Flecks of paint shredded into the syrup.

"Who designed these things, anyway?" he complained. "Is that paint supposed to add vitamins to my peaches?"

"Stop bellyaching!" Hammerlock ordered through a mouthful of food. "The paint just gives it a little texture." He chomped steadily, swallowed, and looked up at Joe. "I can see you don't have the kind of stamina necessary to be a part of our team."

Frank opened a can of Spam. "And just what team is that? The one you've created by kidnapping teenagers?"

The side of the colonel's face that was not paralyzed twitched. "What we have done is not kidnapping," he said with exaggerated calm. "It is merely the recruitment of a new fighting unit—*my fighting unit!*"

Joe noticed that Biff was barely eating. The colonel wiped some food from his lip. "True," he admitted after a long moment. "Some members might come unwillingly. Until they learn how their ability for combat—their individual strength—can be used to change the world."

"Then again," Brand interjected, staring at Lauren and Terry, "some recruits never learn."

Ignoring him, Hammerlock glared across the table at Joe and Frank. "Bureaucratic red tape ruined my military career. The essentials of how that happened are not important. What is important is that I have created an independent fighting unit that does not need to be sanctioned by any government or chain of military command to get a job done!"

Hammerlock continued, becoming more excited by his vision. The more fervent he became, the more he slurred his words.

"We have already begun. Perhaps you read about a strike on an airliner full of hostages taken by terrorists?"

Frank remembered. There had been speculation in the news at the time as to the identity of the rescue force. If his recollection was correct, a number of the hostages had died instead of being saved. And the mysterious rescuers had opened fire on law enforcement officials as well as on the terrorists.

"Oh, yeah, *that* fiasco," Frank said, knowing he was treading on thin ice.

Terry shot him a grin, but Hammerlock's face was mottled with rage. He pounded a fist on the table. "We'd have saved them all if it hadn't been for those pussy-footed police! They interfered with our plan!"

Since the ice was already cracking around him, Frank decided to ask about the San Marcos deal he had read about in the files he'd discovered at the Ultimo Survival Camp.

"You sound indignant and righteous," Frank said, carefully choosing his words. "But if you're so honorable, how could you provide mercenaries to San Marcos? There aren't any high ideals in that kind of business. It's a matter of making profit from human suffering."

Hammerlock stared past the candle flame that fluttered in the space between him and Frank. He slammed down his hand, snuffing out the flame with his palm.

"I don't know what you are talking about," he said in a very quiet voice.

"But I saw—"

Hammerlock cut Frank off. "I will not allow you to sully what I have worked so hard to achieve. The time of my private army has come. My troops do not exist for personal gain. If I discover the location of missing POWs in Vietnam, I will go in with a crack unit at a moment's notice. My men will never negotiate with terrorists. We will deal with a ruthless enemy in a ruthless fashion."

Frank did not back down. "You could end up endangering the lives of hostages, you could end up killing innocent people—have you considered those factors?"

Hammerlock gestured abruptly, stabbing his plastic fork in Frank's direction. "A soldier takes risks with his life. And we are all at war. It won't be long before the public understands this and comes to adore us!"

Joe shook his head in apparent admiration. "Colonel, you are no ordinary man." He paused for a second. "You're a real loony tune!" He pushed his canned peaches away. "Think I'll skip the peaches à la lead poisoning."

Hammerlock looked at Joe as if he were a mutant from outer space. Then he barked out an order to have the table cleared. Orderlies picked up the cans.

Lauren snatched a small package of gum from one of the orderlies. "Just a second, I wasn't finished."

Once the table was cleared, the orderlies returned to deposit a collection of knives in the center of the table. The blades were all sheathed.

Hammerlock picked one up and drew the wicked-looking blade out halfway. "These are Malin M-Fifteen survival knives. Each one contains a precision ZF-Three-sixty Liquid Damped Compass, plus a small survival kit within the handle, including an eighteen-inch cable saw and waterproof matches, among other items."

He shoved the sharp, silvered blade back into the sheath. Metal scraped metal.

"Get up!" Hammerlock ordered.

Joe and Frank supported Biff between them. Biff gamely tried to stand. "I'll be all right," he muttered.

"Just hold on to us for a while, tough guy," Frank murmured.

Hammerlock let the lethal, heavy knife drop to the table. He spoke slowly as if to let every word sink in.

"Recruits, grunts who don't live up to our expectations or who become a threat, get to play our survival game." Hammerlock paused, raising his head from the knives to pierce Terry with his gaze. Terry's eyes did not blink, nor did he look away. "For real!"

Hammerlock picked up the knives and walked around the table, dropping a knife before each of them. "Hunting you down—gives me the chance for a little rest and relaxation."

Terry picked up not only the knife that had been provided for him but Biff's as well. "We'll set you up with this later, Biff."

"You want to get on with it?" Lauren asked coldly.

"The five of you will be set loose in the jungle terrain beyond our fortress." Hammerlock thought for a moment, his expression grave, then nodded, as if in agreement with himself. "I'll give you until dawn and then start after you. I think that's a sporting chance.

"I'll probably be back in time for breakfast, but it will be a pleasant surprise if the five of you are tough enough to make the hunt last until lunch."

Hammerlock drew his Super Blackhawk pistol. He twirled the gun around his forefinger.

"Just consider this the final exam."

Hammerlock suddenly stopped the spinning gun. It was pointed right at Joe's head.

"And I mean just that. You flunk this course—and you die!"

Chapter

12

"THIS IS THE place," Frank Hardy agreed, looking back along the trail. The dawn light rose in a milky haze over the palmetto trees. "If we're going to ambush Hammerlock, we should do it here."

The Hardys, Terry, and Lauren had made their way as quickly as possible along a sandy trail that cut through the scrub and palmetto. They took turns carrying Biff.

Lauren had suggested they use the fireman's carry, straddling Biff over both shoulders. "But how could you—" Joe began.

Lauren answered by slinging Biff over her shoulders and stalking into the woods. They'd had no choice but to follow her.

There was little light among the trees and they

had to watch out for tangled roots twisting up in the sandy path.

Joe followed closely behind Lauren. Hanging over her shoulder, Biff looked back at Joe in desperation.

"You won't tell anyone back home about this, will you?" he pleaded. "Me, saved from death by a girl barely five feet tall."

"They'd have to tear my fingernails out first," Joe assured him. "They'd have to boil me in oil, pluck my eyebrows. And I still wouldn't give them word one."

"Yeah, I've heard that before," Biff said.

Frank nudged Joe, who was staring at Biff, bobbing slightly as Lauren made her way along the path.

"I'll bet Lauren could get it out of you in hree seconds flat," Frank said with a grin.

Joe looked sharply at his brother. He hoped Lauren hadn't heard Frank's comment. She kept walking.

"I saw the way you were looking at her," Frank went on. "Definite interest—maybe even admiration?"

Joe stared at him, exasperated. "Will you shut up? She'll hear you."

Frank shook his head in mild amusement. "In about an hour we're going to have a certifiable homicidal psychopath using us for target practice, and you're worried about what Lauren is going to think."

"Yeah, well, you're the one who brought her up. Are you just jealous because she likes me better than you?" Joe asked.

"Oh, right, can't you see my heart is breaking?" Frank replied. "Lauren," he called, putting an end to the conversation. "Why don't you let me take Biff for a while?"

With seemingly no effort Lauren transferred Biff to Frank's shoulders.

"You've go to stop eating all those burgers, Biff!" Frank grunted as they started off again.

They discussed possible scenarios against Hammerlock as the sky slowly brightened. Frank was the strategist.

"I think the major thing that we have to keep reminding ourselves is that we can't afford a physical confrontation with Hammerlock. He's skilled at this sort of hunting and far stronger."

"So, what you're saying," Joe said as he accepted Biff on his shoulders, "is that our only chance is to outwit him."

It was just before dawn. They knew they had fifteen minutes at most before Hammerlock would set out after them.

"Maybe we should set some sort of ambush for him. No one, outside the colonel and his elite squad, lives on this island," said Terry.

"We have no idea how far away the next Caribbean Island is," Frank continued with the planning, "so there's no reason to head for the beach, which is what I'm sure he'll expect us to try. We just can't chance swimming, without knowing how far and in what direction the closest inhabited island is."

Lauren picked the actual spot in the trail where they would stage their ambush. "You see how the trail zigzags here very sharply. So when Hammerlock approaches this point, he's blind to anyone stationed nearby."

Joe looked excitedly into her vivid blue eyes. Her pupils seemed to enlarge slightly.

"You've got a plan!" he said with a note of triumph. He turned to Frank. "I love it! She beat you to the punch!"

Frank rolled his eyes.

"You haven't heard my plan yet," Lauren reminded him coolly.

Joe nodded. "That's true. But when I do, I know I'm going to love it!"

Lauren tried not to smile and failed. Turning to Frank, she asked, "Is he always like this?"

"Only when his life is in danger," Frank replied.

Terry disappeared while they were working out the actual logistics of the trap.

"I'm not sure I like this," Frank said as the sky began to turn a light peach color.

"What's wrong, Frank?" Lauren asked as she inspected a tree near the edge of the path. She was going to climb up one trunk, and Terry another, in the hopes that they could drop down on the colonel when he passed below.

"I'll tell you," Joe said, picking a spot alongside the path where the scrub brush was densest and would make the best hiding place. "Frank doesn't like the idea of us taking direct physical action against Hammerlock."

"Let's say I have a few reservations," Frank said grimly.

"Look at it this way, Frank. What we've really done is combine our collective intelligence with force," Joe reasoned.

"It sounds good when you put it that way," Frank admitted grudgingly.

Lauren tested the lower branches of the tree. She nodded to herself. The branches would support her.

Then she turned to Frank. "I think our best bet at this point is to try to put Hammerlock on the defensive," she explained, her sapphire eyes thoughtful. "He's bound to think we'll be concentrating on finding a way off his human game preserve."

Biff was hidden deep in a thicket off to the side of the trail. He seemed stronger than when the boys had first found him, but he was still weak and bruised from the beatings.

"I'm reduced to being a mere 'spotter,' " he grumbled.

Frank studied the sky. "Sun's up. Hammerlock

must be on his way by now. It won't be long."

Joe whirled about, looking left and right, obviously disturbed.

"What's wrong, Joe?" Lauren asked.

"Terry! Where's Terry? Anybody see him?" His voice rose in concern.

"Calm down, Joe." Terry's voice came from the trees. He appeared a moment later, carrying all their canteens.

"Where'd you go? What'd you take our canteens for?" Joe asked.

Terry handed Joe one of the canteens. "Try some of this."

As Terry pushed through the brush to hand a canteen to Biff, Joe unscrewed the cap. He took a sniff. "What is it?" he asked, wrinkling his nose.

"It's a drink made from crushed cinnamon, ginger, and a special tree bark," Terry replied. "Drink up. It's actually good, and it'll give you strength." Terry caught Joe looking distrustfully at his canteen. "Stop making faces, Joe. Set a good example for Biff."

Terry silently worked his way through the thicket, back out onto the path. "Hammerlock won't expect any of us to know how to live off what's at hand on this island. This puts us one up on him already."

Joe took a cautious sip. "Hey, this isn't so bad, after all."

"How'd you learn to make this?" Frank asked.

"I told you my dad was an agent. He was

stationed in the Caribbean for a while when I was a kid, and he taught me how to make it. I guess he was doing some kind of counterinsurgency stuff. He never talked much about it," Terry answered as he studied the tree he was to climb.

"Time to get ready," Frank said when he had finished the exotic drink. "Take your places."

Lauren climbed nimbly up the tree she had chosen. She had her knife drawn, and for an instant sunlight glinted off the razor-sharp metal.

"Watch it!" Joe called up to her. "Hammerlock could spot that."

She realized what had happened and scraped the knife blade against the bark of the tree to dull the shine. "Sorry," she said in a whisper. "I didn't realize. And you'd better keep your voice down, or he'll hear us for sure."

Joe gave her a thumbs-up sign and whispered, "Now we're even."

As Joe settled himself in the brush, he had an odd sense of déjà vu. Why? It came to him suddenly. Except for the fact that there were fronds and scrub and sand, the act of lying in wait reminded him of the night he and Frank and Biff and Tony Prito had played their survival game in Bayport.

It seemed a lifetime ago.

Biff had given the signal, a circular wave of his hand. The thickets were silent, the ambushers holding their collective breath as Hammerlock moved toward the bend in the trail. He came into sight, then stood motionless.

Listening.

Eyes searching.

Hammerlock wore a torn olive-drab safari shirt. His bulging arms were smeared with black and green camouflage paint. He pressed himself up against a tree trunk, almost willing himself to become a part of it.

Come on! Move! Joe thought, trying to will him to take three more steps. That would place him right between the two Hardys.

What's stopping him? Some sixth sense? Joe wondered.

Hammerlock sprang away from the tree, moving all in a rush. He was going to run right by them. It all happened so abruptly that Joe was afraid Hammerlock would be past and gone before they could spring the trap. He pushed himself outward, ready to wrap his arms around the colonel's strong midsection. His hands slid on greased flesh. He couldn't hold on!

Hammerlock had expected the attack. He was already whirling away from it, flinging Joe into the scrub. His pistol appeared in his hand, as if from nowhere, and the barrel erupted with flame. The gun sounded like a cannon.

He had aimed up at the tree where Terry was stationed. The .44-caliber bullet tore the limb from beneath Terry's feet!

Terry gasped, clawing at branches, anything to

stop his fall. He plunged downward, hit a branch, and tumbled into the scrub near where Joe had hidden.

Hammerlock spun around, his attention back on Joe. His gun was lowered, ready to fire again.

Now the weapon that had pulverized the tree limb was aimed directly at the bridge of Joe's nose. He was as good as dead, no doubt about it! Hammerlock couldn't miss at this range.

Joe took a deep breath.

Lauren landed on Hammerlock's back, booted feet first. The blow would have knocked a normal man to the ground. But not Hammerlock. The shock just knocked his gun hand a few inches off. The gun exploded with flame and thunder and the bullet whizzed by just above Joe's head.

She saved my life! Joe thought, diving off the trail. How can I ever make it up to her?

Lauren hit the sandy path, rolling into the scrub. She came up fast and was running immediately. Joe found her right beside him as he hurtled through the jungle foliage.

"I thought I was dead!" he told her.

"I thought you were, too," she answered.

"How'd he know where we were?" Joe asked furiously. "It isn't fair! One moment, we had him dead. And then the next second, he's on to us!" Almost, he thought, as if someone had told him.

"I just hope Frank and Terry are all right," Lauren said as they reached Biff.

"It was a fiasco, huh?" he asked.

"A *complete* fiasco," Joe admitted.

Frank Hardy's heart hammered in his chest as he ran. Hammerlock was gaining on him. And Frank knew it!

Frank crushed roots underfoot and shoved branches out of his way as he tore through the underbrush. In spite of the obstacles, he was making top speed in the mad race. Only problem is, Frank thought, I'm blazing a trail for Hammerlock!

Frank reached the far side of a palmetto thicket. He stopped and bent over, breathing heavily, his hands on his knees. He saw an open space ahead of him. Got to get across that, find a place to hide. At least I can make some speed here.

He made himself begin running again.

It was a mistake.

Frank knew it immediately.

His feet sank into a quagmire. It quickly oozed up past the tops of his boots. He tried to yank himself free. But the bog held on to his legs like a thousand leeches, refusing to let go.

Behind him in the thicket, he could hear Hammerlock approaching.

A bitter taste filled Frank's mouth. Perfect—a choice of deaths! Sink slowly until this quicksand strangles me, or let Hammerlock blow me away!

Chapter

13

THE QUICKSAND WAS the consistency and color of maple syrup, and it clung tenaciously to Frank.

His first panicked efforts to pull himself free had resulted in pushing him in deeper, up to his thighs. Mud slipped inside his boots, like cold worms crawling past his socks to his feet.

Hammerlock had stopped running. Frank could imagine him, just beyond the patch of quicksand, standing very still as he had on the trail. He would be listening, trying to figure out why Frank wasn't making any more noise.

Perhaps he expected another trap. He would proceed cautiously.

That would give Frank a few precious extra seconds. But for what purpose? If Hammerlock discovered him stuck helplessly, he only had to stand and watch until the ooze slid over Frank's head and bubbled with his last tortured breaths. Or he could use Frank for target practice. Knowing Hammerlock, Frank fully expected to be used as target practice.

Even though he had stopped moving, the quicksand had managed to suck Frank down to his waist. Looking around frantically, he raised his hands so they would not become trapped.

Snap!

Hammerlock was on the move again. Slowly, but on the move!

And heading directly toward Frank!

Frank's hands reached back, searching desperately above his head. They closed over something wooden. A branch? What? He twisted around to see, sending himself deeper into the quicksand.

He had grabbed onto a set of palmetto roots, hanging over the embankment, and thrusting down into the quicksand.

Another footfall, quieter this time. No snap of wood, just a slight squeezing noise, a bending of grass underfoot. He wouldn't have heard it if Hammerlock had not been so close.

Think, Frank! Think! You're always telling Joe to analyze a situation. Make the most of whatever is at hand, Frank said to himself.

But what was at hand? Quicksand that would clutch at his hands and hold them prisoner. Palmetto roots that had been arcing down into the quicksand depths for decades.

And then he had a vision of his girlfriend, Callie Shaw, back in Bayport. Could it be just a few days before that they'd been swimming in the clear water of the ocean? The idea came to him just then.

Maybe he could convince Hammerlock that he had *already* died. Frank grabbed hold of the palmetto roots and started to push himself down, down, under the slime.

Holding tightly on to the roots, Frank started making as much noise as he could, twisting and thrashing in the mud.

Hand over hand he forced himself down into the muck. Up to his chest. Clammy goo slid wetly under his armpits. Up to his chin!

He couldn't do it. His brain fought too hard against him.

Suppose you can't pull yourself back up, he thought. Suppose you only think you can. Suppose you force yourself under, and the ooze enters your mouth, and your nostrils, and you suffocate? If you can't pull yourself free, what then?

You cannot do this, he told himself.

He heard Hammerlock, just on the other side of the palmetto trees. Two, three steps at the most. Then the colonel would be standing over him, aiming that gun. He forgot what the name of it was, but he remembered Hammerlock telling him what it could do to a water buffalo!

He pulled himself under.

The muck squeezed over his head. It ran into his ears. It tried to force its way past his closed eyelids. It seeped between his clenched lips. He could taste grit against his tongue, feel it grind between his teeth. Mud spread slowly into the back of his throat. He was gagging!

Then his hands began slipping on the muck-covered roots!

Pull yourself up! Pull yourself up! his mind screamed.

No! Not yet. Please, not yet. Maybe Hammerlock is standing up there, watching the spot where the mud closed over your head.

His fingers were growing numb, aching. Mud seeped into his nostrils. He tried to exhale and force it out, but somehow the stuff managed to flow in deeper.

He couldn't wait any longer!

He wanted to reach up, to grasp higher, almost afraid to let go of the root. He threw his hand up and it slid. It slid down!

In the darkness, behind his tightly closed eyelids, he could feel his blood pounding. The darkness of the mud pressed in on him relentlessly. It was getting hard to concentrate. Which way was up? The pounding in his chest grew fiercer. He felt as if he'd breathed flames into his lungs. They were burning!

He forced his arm up again, forced his fingers to close tightly around the slippery root.

I've got to breathe! My lungs are going to burst, he thought, his mind beginning to race.

He could feel blood rushing in his temples.

Mud oozed deeper into his ears. Mud was everywhere! He was never going to get out.

He yanked himself upward, fiercely. His head thrust up through the quagmire. Rivulets of muck slid down from his hair, over his forehead. Frank yanked ferociously on the tangled root. Now his nose and lips were free. Coughing, nearly choking, he finally drew in a sobbing breath. Air! Fresh air!

Straining, battling the unyielding pull of the quicksand, he finally reached a dry area.

I beat you! he thought fiercely as if the bog were a living enemy.

Frank was almost afraid he'd look up to see Hammerlock's gun pointed at his head. Finally he forced himself to see if he was alone—and took a long, shaky breath. He was.

As he pulled himself free he felt another surge of triumph over the swamp and the mud.

He crawled into the grass and lay there, gasping. He knew he had to get back to Joe and the others. But he needed just a few moments to breathe, to wipe his hands clean, to try to get the mud out of his ears and mouth.

He was still lying in the tall swamp grass, his breathing getting back to normal, when he heard the voices. Frank lay still, listening to the sounds of several bodies forcing their way through the palmetto thicket.

"Let's hurry this up," one voice said. "I heard gunshots coming from over here somewhere."

Frank peered through the grass, to see Major Brand carrying a submachine gun. Two of the counselors from the Ultimo Survival Camp accompanied him. They, too, were armed.

Brand checked the action on his weapon as he passed within six feet of Frank's head. He never noticed his quarry. The mud on Frank's body acted as a natural camouflage.

"Those grunts and Hammerlock can't be far ahead." Brand laughed. It sounded shockingly loud in the quiet jungle. "Let's finish up this turkey shoot. Then we can take our cool million!"

He snapped the action of his gun, then led his team onward. They moved confidently, crashing through the brush, not even trying to hide their progress.

Frank managed to get to his feet. He clung to one of the palmetto trees.

He had to warn Joe and the others! He had to reach them in time!

And he had to do it without running into at least four people who wanted him dead!

Chapter

14

THE HARDEST THING for Joe Hardy to do was to keep his imagination from dwelling on the ways Frank might die if Hammerlock caught him.

He worked beside Terry and Lauren on a new trap they had talked about as a backup for their first trap. They had planned it back when Frank was still with them, before their ambush had failed so disastrously. How had it gone so wrong? How had Hammerlock known where they were? Joe had difficulty concentrating on the hard work at hand.

At any second, he kept expecting to hear gunshots in the distance—abrupt, brief, and fatal for his brother.

If he had any idea in which direction Frank had fled, he would have attempted to follow. But he didn't have a clue. His last glimpse of Frank had been during the brief scuffle with Hammerlock, before they'd all taken off running. He and Lauren had picked up Biff. Then they'd found Terry crouching in the brush, some distance from the tree where he'd almost been shot. The severed branch had saved him from a full impact with the ground.

"Frank!" Joe had said nervously, looking around. "Where's Frank?"

Terry had shaken his head. "I'm sorry, Joe. I don't know. I hit the ground hard, and people were running all around me. I thought Hammerlock would appear at any moment, aim that cannon of his at me, and that would be it! Bye-bye time."

Terry had paused, and his almond eyes had expressed his pain and sorrow even before he spoke. "Hammerlock didn't chase you, or Biff, or Lauren, or me. There's only one target left, I'm afraid."

"Frank," Joe whispered numbly.

They had searched briefly for some clue as to where Frank might have fled. But the jungle kept its secret. They had no idea when—or if—Frank would return.

Joe's mind kept returning to the one thought: How? How could Hammerlock have known they were there?

He reconstructed the ambush in his head. Two images kept haunting him. Lauren, high in the tree, her knife shining in the sunlight. An accident? he asked himself. Then there was Terry, disappearing into the jungle to get the supplies for his survival punch. But gone long enough to give us away, he thought.

Joe shook his head. You can't think like this. You're depending on these people to help save your life. Another thought pushed its way forward. They may already have cost Frank his life. Joe squashed that thought, too. They had to start work on the second trap. They *had* to.

As he and Terry picked out the two small trees they would use to build their trap, memories of Frank plagued Joe. He could hear his brother's voice, as clearly as if it were real, saying he would back him no matter what. He saw Frank's face, looking at him with concern, when Frank had thought he really fell down the mountainside.

Then came the nightmare memory that always surfaced when he was upset. A vision of the moment their car had exploded, with his girlfriend, Iola Morton, caught inside. Joe had not saved her. He had failed Iola—as he had just failed Frank.

Come on, get to work, Joe told himself. This is what Frank would have wanted you to do. But the thought gave him little comfort.

He and Terry twisted open the tops of the handles of their Malin M-15 survival knives. They each withdrew the wire saws coiled within. They were really ingenious little gizmos—eighteen inches long, with razor-sharp teeth.

Joe hooked one of the saw's ringlike grips over his finger, then dug out the nylon fishing cords tucked tightly inside the handle. Terry did the same, placing them beside the trunks of the chosen trees.

Terry stretched the nylon cord between his hands and tugged. The line bit into the palms of his hands. He pulled harder. His flesh creased more deeply, but the line held firm.

"It'll hold," Terry said.

Joe barely heard. He was still brooding about Frank. If Joe survived this thing and Frank didn't, how would he explain it to their parents? He imagined his mother fighting back tears. Joe's own eyes began to sting and fill. He quickly blinked back the tears before the others could see them.

Terry began to use the saw on one of the small trees, carving notches into the bark. Joe halfheartedly ripped his saw's teeth across the second trunk. Could he have given us away? he asked himself.

Lauren stopped beside him. Sunlight glinted off her blond hair.

"You all right?" she asked, standing above him as he watched wood shavings spew away from the saw.

"Yes," he said, but did not mean it. That knife reflecting the sun. A dead giveaway, Joe thought.

Lauren knelt beside him. Her clear blue eyes were full of concern.

"I have a lot of brothers and sisters," she said after long seconds in which the only sound was the saws chewing through wood.

"So you said." Joe stopped sawing, glanced up into her eyes, then turned away.

"I may have wanted to do something to prove myself, apart from them. But if one of them were hurt—if something happened to *any* of them, I don't know what I'd do. I'd be lost." She paused. "Please, don't blame youself."

"It's *my* problem," he muttered. The saw stuck in the wood, and he jerked at it savagely.

Lauren grabbed his arm, stopped him. One hand touched his cheek and turned his face back to her.

She smiled grimly. "No, Joe. It's *our* problem. We're all a team here. We're working together. It's the only way we'll get out of this alive."

Joe's voice was sarcastic. "You sound like a football coach giving a pep talk."

Lauren smiled. "Maybe. But I wouldn't give up on your brother. From what I've seen, he's pretty resourceful. I'm betting he'll outwit Hammerlock."

The day became instantly warmer. Joe knew it was only because of Lauren.

"You're right. I shouldn't be counting Frank out," Joe said.

He stared into her eyes, and found himself liking Lauren for her never-say-die spirit and her compassion. "I—" he began.

And then he felt a sudden sharp stab of guilt. Iola. The explosion.

The day went cold again, as if he had betrayed Iola's memory. She had been the only girl he'd ever really cared about. Could anyone ever really take her place?

"Joe, are you okay?" Lauren asked. "You just stopped speaking so quickly. And you look so—hurt. What is it?"

He couldn't look directly at her, so he went back to sawing notches in the tree. "There's no time to discuss it now. I wouldn't know what to say about it, anyway," he answered evasively.

He changed the subject. "I still keep wondering how Hammerlock could have tumbled to us so quickly. He zeroed in on us like a homing pigeon coming to roost. The man's incredible!"

"He is that!" Lauren said, standing. The mention of Hammerlock's name made her nervous.

She clapped Joe on the shoulder. "Now, let me get to work."

Terry stopped sawing and looked over at them. "Good. For a while there I thought I was going to have to set this trap all by myself."

He surveyed the notches he had carved into the small tree. "I think this one is finished. Let me help you, Joe." Terry came over to them. He stopped beside Lauren and grinned. "But first, coach, have you got a pep talk for me, too?"

"Do you need one?" she asked.

"Hey, everybody can use a good pep talk once

in a while." He patted her on the shoulder. "Go carve your spear. When Joe and I are done here, we'll come over and help you."

"Thanks, Terry," she said, moving rapidly through the shrubs toward a thin sapling.

"She's okay," Terry said admiringly.

Joe looked up. "So are you, Terry."

"We've got a good group here." Terry pointed to where Biff was keeping a lookout some distance away. "Including Biff. The three of us got to know each other pretty well. You have a lot of time for talk when you're locked up together. Look at him out there, totally vigilant. Even hurt, he still wants to pull his weight. Hammerlock won't be able to sneak past him." Terry knelt beside Joe. "Okay, let's get this job finished."

They carved notches on either side of the tree. After a bit, they pulled on the tree, bending it backward. The thin tree pulled against their hands. It had a lot of tension and wanted to spring upright.

"That'll do the trick," Terry said.

"I think you're right," Joe said. He felt better, but he was still waiting for the jungle air to be ripped apart by gunshots. What if I'm wrong? he wondered. One of these two may already have gotten Frank killed.

It took Lauren less than five minutes to saw through the sapling. She coiled the thin metal saw back into its original shape and forced it into the handle of the knife. She held the knife with great care. It was a weapon to respect.

When she was in the middle of carving the spear out of the sapling, Joe and Terry joined her. They helped her trim and carve the spear tip.

The sun was climbing high above the trees now, and the sky was clear, so beautiful that it seemed to promise paradise.

They finished the spear. It ended in a jagged, rough-hewn point, the pale gleaming yellow of freshly cut wood.

Lauren stared at Biff. He was still waiting. No signal.

Hammerlock was not yet ready to attack again.

The three of them forced the small, notched trees backward until their tops touched the ground. They fastened the bent trees in firing position with the nylon fishing cords. They all held their breath, hoping the cords would hold the trees in check—until the time came to fire. The cords stretched, but held.

They were nocking the spear into the center of the line stretched between the trees, but had not completed the task, when Biff signaled emphatically from his vantage point.

"It's Hammerlock!" Lauren said. "And he's close."

"Real close," Joe agreed, a sick feeling in his stomach. "He found us again—thirty seconds before we're ready."

Chapter

15

BIFF REMAINED STILL, watching Hammerlock's confident advance. Hammerlock would pass within ten yards of him. Biff gritted his teeth. There was no way he could stop Hammerlock. He was still too weak to defend even himself. He could only watch—and warn the others.

The colonel held the powerful handgun at his side, straight down. In seconds, though, Biff knew he could whip it up, aim, and fire.

It would be insane for Biff to let Hammerlock know where he was hidden among the covering of thick fronds. But a glance over his shoulder told him that Joe and the others did not yet have the spear nocked in place. Hammerlock would be upon them before they could get it ready for firing.

Biff's hands searched quickly over the sand for rocks. He found one! Two! A third!

Hammerlock was almost past him. In ten seconds, tops, he would spot the threesome.

It was now or never.

Biff raised himself painfully, afraid his legs wouldn't support him. He shook, like an invalid standing for the first time in years.

Can't let myself fall, he thought.

His knees buckled and pain shot up his legs, deep into his thighs, and he started to topple.

Hammerlock heard the noise and went into a quick crouch, turning at the same instant. His gun hand came up, just as quickly as Biff had known it would!

"What is he doing? Has he gone nuts?" Joe asked in stunned disbelief. The sick feeling wouldn't go away. Somehow, Hammerlock knew how to find us again. Terry or Lauren must be on his side, Joe thought.

Biff fell against the side of the tree. It was the only thing holding him up. Hammerlock was moving toward Biff, zeroing in on his prey.

Joe could see that Biff had something in his fists. He was raising one of his arms.

Rocks! He has rocks, Joe thought, horrified. Rocks against state-of-the-art weaponry!

It was like watching a modern David and Goliath, Biff so vulnerable and small against the mighty figure of Hammerlock!

"Come on!" Terry said. "He's buying us time. Let's not waste it!"

Hammerlock's gun fired, and Joe heard Biff cry out.

The bullet tore a chunk out of the tree just half an inch from Biff's head. It would have hit him if he had not lurched when he threw the rock. The rock landed short of Hammerlock.

Biff knew he was going to fall. His legs were giving out on him. He tossed the second rock, giving it everything he had, and plunged forward, falling through leaves and branches.

With a moan of pain, he rolled, crushing vegetation that was in his way. He suddenly wondered if there were poisonous snakes on this island. Who cares, he thought, I'm going to get a bullet in the head any second now.

He rolled in the direction of the spear trap. If he was going to buy it, the best he could do was lead Hammerlock in its direction—make *Hammerlock* the target of the day, for once!

Biff sprawled out in front of the trajectory area for the spear. He could hear Hammerlock coming after him.

Keep your head low, Biff told himself, or you'll end up as the first piece of shish kebab.

Hammerlock appeared five feet away from him, his figure blotting out the trees and sun. He aimed his gun at Biff.

If the spear-slingshot wasn't ready, Biff was as good as dead!

* * *

Joe glared at Terry as they cut the nylon restraining cords. If he sabotages us now, I'll know, Joe thought. But the trees whipped upward. The spear was shot forward like a giant arrow. All three watched, mesmerized, as it sailed over Biff's sprawled, helpless form.

Hammerlock's head snapped up. The huge gun followed as quickly. The unparalyzed side of his face reacted to the sight of the spear rushing at him.

The spear caught Hammerlock before he could move! It hit him high in the shoulder and knocked him off his feet. The carved wood broke as he landed, cracking in half with a tearing sound.

Joe leapt to his feet.

"*Got him!*"

The huge body rolled and closed in on itself.

"*We've won!*"

Joe rushed forward. Lauren and Terry were on either side of him.

Hammerlock moved. Joe could not believe it, but the colonel was pushing himself up onto his hands and knees. The three of them came to a stop, frozen in disbelief.

Impossible! Joe told himself. No man could get up after that!

Like some mythical monster, Hammerlock rose to his feet, the broken spear still protruding from his safari shirt. His good eye looked down at it as if it were only a minor nuisance. One greased hand reached up, gripped the broken spear, and ripped it free. He disdainfully tossed it into the sand, and then turned his attention to the three- some standing no more than a dozen yards away.

Terry did his best to nail Hammerlock, thought Joe. So Lauren had to be the traitor. He turned to her.

But Lauren was charging Hammerlock. Joe could scarcely believe it. She covered half a dozen yards, moving without a word, her knife held tight in her hand. She would never make it. He knew she would never make it! "No!" he screamed, but he was too late.

The Super Blackhawk came up, fired. The bul- let caught Lauren, whipping her about violently. She hit the sand with a muted thud and lay there motionless.

Hammerlock walked deliberately toward them, callously stepping over Lauren's inert body. He didn't even give her a second glance.

Joe was gasping for breath. He felt as if every- thing he had ever feared had finally caught up with him.

Iola. Frank. Now Lauren. Dead! All of them, dead!

He stared into Hammerlock's emotionless face and felt the rage build within him. He could hardly hold himself still. All he wanted was a crack at this psychopath! Just one chance to even the score!

"Hey, Hammerlock," he called to the colonel. "You want a fight? A fair fight? Why not put that gun down and go one on one with me?" Although he was seething with fury, Joe's voice was cold.

Hammerlock's face never changed expression as he studied Joe. "That's a laugh. What is it with you, kid? You go to the movies a lot or something? I'm not going to risk anything. When you've got an enemy cornered, you kill him. And that's exactly what I'm going to do to you. I'm going to shoot you stone-cold *dead*."

Joe stood his ground, Terry beside him.

Hammerlock raised his gun to firing position, wincing as he did so. "That was a cute idea, using those trees as a bow. Too bad it didn't work."

The colonel tapped his chest where the spear had hit. "I'm wearing a Kevlar vest under my shirt. Your spear hurt, but it didn't penetrate." His voice was deadly quiet, and did not reflect pain. "I don't like being hurt."

Hammerlock moved the huge gun until its barrel was aimed directly between Joe's eyes.

"For what it's worth," Joe said, trying to breathe evenly, "I don't like having guns pointed at me. How about if that makes us even?"

"Not a chance," Hammerlock answered. His thick forefinger started to squeeze the trigger!

Chapter

16

LAUREN MADIGAN FELT the blood trickle warmly down her side.

The force of the bullet had given her whole body a tremendous shock, even though it had only grazed her side. She had known she could never reach Hammerlock with the knife. But she had never really intended to. She just wanted him to think she had.

It had all been a matter of timing. She had watched Hammerlock's fingers, trying to anticipate the second the trigger would be pulled. When she was positive he was about to shoot, she had whipped her body about, hoping that she would be out of the trajectory of the bullet, but that it would *look* as if it had hit her.

She didn't quite make it—yet she had been partially successful. The bullet had actually grazed her, and she hadn't had to fake her hard collision with the sand.

She hadn't even had to concentrate on remaining motionless. The initial trauma to her nervous system took care of that. Even a minor wound from a high-caliber weapon such as Hammerlock's caused a devastating reaction to the body. No acting was needed.

By the time Hammerlock stepped over her, she was becoming aware again of the sand and voices.

From the corner of her eye, Lauren could see Biff valiantly, but hopelessly, crawling through the sand. He was too far away to reach Hammerlock in time, and too weak to do anything even if he did.

She looked past Hammerlock and caught a glimpse of Terry trying to position his knife for an underhanded throw. He was trying not to make an overt movement, or Hammerlock would spot it and squeeze off half a dozen shots in two seconds. And he had them dead in his sights.

But Lauren could fix that. She kicked out, straight and hard. Her booted heel thrust into Hammerlock's leg, right behind the knee. The leg gave, and for a split second Hammerlock's pistol wavered.

Joe and Terry were upon him instantly. Joe dove high, his fist slamming into Hammerlock's throat. Terry hit the colonel's broad midsection. They all tumbled into the sand.

Lauren joined the melee, sending a hard right hook into Hammerlock's nose.

Joe was throwing punches, anywhere he could land a fist, when he heard someone laugh. He had heard that laugh before—that hideous laugh that sounded like bones scraping together.

Hammerlock took advantage of the instant's distraction. He flung Joe away like a rag doll, and was lurching back onto his feet when he heard the laugh again.

"Playing in the sand, Colonel?" the voice asked.

Everyone became still.

Orville Brand. Brand with an automatic weapon. Brand smiling, there to claim his prize.

He wasn't alone. There were two other paramilitary types with him. And they were both armed.

Joe glared at Brand, ready to charge him.

The major's dark, sunken eyes appraised Joe, his machine gun aimed at Joe's chest.

"What a pleasure to see you looking so well," Brand said tauntingly.

Hammerlock disengaged himself from Terry and Lauren.

"Sporting chance, huh?" Joe spat at Hammerlock with contempt. "You come after us with superior firepower, and even then you need backup troops to cover for you."

The left side of Hammerlock's face twitched. "You condemn me unjustly. I didn't order Brand or any of these others to give me strike support."

Hammerlock glared at Brand. "You're getting overzealous. You know I go on these hunts alone. How dare you disregard the procedure? You'd better have a good excuse, Major."

Hammerlock stalked heavily over to the spot where his Super Blackhawk pistol had landed. He started to bend to pick it up.

"Colonel," Brand said, his tone part command, part warning.

Puzzled, Hammerlock cocked his head in Brand's direction. Then he saw that the machine gun was aimed at him.

"I wouldn't," Brand said.

Hammerlock stood very still, trying to understand what was happening. He took a threatening step toward Brand, and the other two men swung their weapons to cover him.

Hammerlock stopped dead. He was too much the seasoned warrior to move, knowing that the odds were against him.

Hammerlock ignored the others, staring only at Brand. "Am I to understand that you are like those bureaucrats who betrayed me so many years ago? Am I to understand that the bonds that held us together in the face of war have been destroyed?"

"So, the death game comes full circle," Joe said mockingly.

Hammerlock stared at Brand in honest bewilderment. "I saved your life," he said.

"That was a long time ago," Brand replied. "You couldn't possibly expect subservience forever."

"Subservience, no, but loyalty, yes!" Hammerlock snarled.

"Brand believes in money more than loyalty, right, Major?" Joe asked sarcastically. He was thinking of the documents Frank had found.

"It's the San Marcos business, isn't it?" Joe continued. "Hammerlock was telling the truth when he denied knowing anything about that mercenary deal." He shook his head. "He *is* a psychopath, who thinks there are simple answers to complex world problems. But at least he's not out to make big bucks from them."

"Is that true, Orville?" Hammerlock asked. His face became unreadable again.

"Why don't you give me a harangue about honor, Colonel? Honor is an illusion. It's in your mind. It's a disease that has prevented you from seeing how what we created could make us rich men!" Brand's anger seemed to get the better of him, and Joe was afraid he might open fire.

"I created Ultimo," Hammerlock stated, but it was in a dead voice, as if he had already decided the argument was over.

"But *I'm* going to turn the squadron into the highest-paid independent mercenary unit ever,"

Brand informed him. "With or without Ultimo. In a little over two weeks, I'm going to take command of our forces and lead them in a strike into San Marcos."

Hammerlock's guttural voice was devoid of threat, just flat and distant. "I'll never let you turn this noble fighting unit into a collection of hyenas and jackals."

Brand shrugged. "Yes. That's the problem. You see, Colonel, I wish I could leave you here on this island to play your little games, but I know you would oppose me."

"You should know that. You've known me long enough."

"The troops have been training for this operation and this operation alone. They think you approve of it." Brand's dark, sunken eyes shone. "If I let you return to camp, you could create tremendous divisiveness within the troops. Right now, as long as they think you endorse it, they're hungry to go into battle."

"Over my dead body," Hammerlock said.

Brand's thin lips parted in a smile. "Exactly, Colonel."

Terry picked himself up, anticipating what was coming. "Oh, and let me guess," he said. "You're going to use us as the scapegoats. You're going to make it look like one of us killed the colonel during his little foray."

"Brilliant, Terry," Brand said. "Your father

would be proud of you. Of course, he'll never know."

"Because we'll all be dead. You'll have had to avenge the dear colonel," Terry said.

Brand nodded. "Yes. That should make you happy, Colonel. The troops will love the revenge angle. You've trained them so efficiently on the subject." Brand paused, then added, "And, of course, in the end, I will make over a million dollars."

Brand aimed his machine gun at Joe. One of the other men kept Hammerlock covered. The third man aimed at Terry.

Biff started crawling again. He shouted, "No!" but no one bothered to react to him.

Brand's thin lips pulled up over his large teeth. "Looks like you're on the firing range again, Joseph! Only this time there are no wooden targets. Game's over." He nodded toward the other men. "Ready on the firing line. Ready!" A dramatic pause for effect, and then the command, "Aim!"

Chapter

17

"FI—"

Frank Hardy's boots slammed into Brand's mouth, driving the last command down his throat. Brand fell backward, Frank on top of him. Frank's hands went for Brand's machine gun, trying to wrest it from him.

"Go for Hammerlock's gun, Joe! Get the gun!" Frank shouted. The machine gun in his hands quivered like a living thing as he grappled with Brand, its barrel swaying back and forth before his face. If Brand got his finger inside the trigger guard, Frank's plan would turn into another disaster.

Frank had heard the gunfire, which told both Brand and him where the colonel was located. Then he had followed Brand and company, climbing a tree while Brand confronted Hammerlock. All the time Frank kept trying to figure out the best plan of attack against four weapons when he had none!

Brand had forced the issue, with his decision to carry out an on-the-spot execution. Frank had to do something immediately.

He had tensed his muscles for the jump, choosing his target. It had to be Brand. Frank knew Joe would go into action, and he suspected that Lauren and Terry would do the same. Even Hammerlock should be on their side in the resulting skirmish.

When Frank and Brand tumbled into the sand, the two mercenaries looked around in confusion, as if trying to decide whom to shoot first. They did not have more than a couple of seconds to consider.

Joe dove wildly, hit the sand on his right shoulder, grabbed Hammerlock's pistol in the middle of a roll, and came up on one knee. The gun felt heavy and gritty with sand.

Hammerlock elbowed the mercenary nearest him in the stomach and had that man's weapon in his hands before Joe was in a firing position. The last soldier swung his gun toward Hammerlock, but the huge man was gone, swallowed up by the jungle.

Terry hurled himself into the other soldier with a jolting body block that sent the man and weapon flying.

The man Terry had hit lay curled up on the

ground, gurgling. He did not look as if he would want to move for a long, long time.

Brand was up, bashing Frank's hands against a sand-covered rock. Once! Twice! Frank tried to hold on to the weapon, but once he realized it was useless, he let go and scrambled away. Brand tried to bring the weapon to bear on Frank, but thought better of it when Joe snapped off a shot with the Super Blackhawk.

The gun's heavy recoil shook Joe's gun hand, jerking it up.

Before he could get off another shot, Brand thrashed away into the jungle. They could hear him running.

Joe looked at the gun in his hand with new respect.

Frank got to his feet, rubbing his knuckles where Brand had battered them. Joe ran over to him.

"Miss me?" Frank asked with a grin.

Frank was the color of mud, from head to toe.

Joe looked him over in disbelief. "You look like a walking lump of oatmeal."

"That's a nice way to talk to someone who just saved your life."

Joe hugged him fiercely. "I don't care if I do get crud all over me!"

Terry ran up to them, holding one of the machine guns. His face was glowing with victory.

"I can't believe we did it!" he shouted, and then all three were hugging one another.

"Someone keep telling me, 'I'm alive! I'm alive!' " Lauren said, joining the group.

Terry spoke excitedly. "When that spear got Hammerlock and he just yanked it out, I told myself, 'It can't be.' And then when he aimed his gun at you"—he shook Joe happily—"I've got to tell you, I didn't figure your chances were very hot."

Joe grinned. "Imagine how *I* felt." He took a deep breath. We all fought Hammerlock. We're all on the same side!

Terry backed away from the group, wiping mud off his clothes. He took a long look at Frank.

"Frank," he said, "you're a mess."

He smiled. "Yeah. But we made Hammerlock miss his breakfast."

Lauren gave a good imitation of being contrite. "Yes, I feel bad about that." She broke into a laugh of relief. "But I think I can get over it."

Joe noticed the wet bloodstain on Lauren's side. "How bad is it?" he asked, worried.

"Not bad," she replied gamely, but he knew it hurt.

"We should get you patched up. Let's take a seat over here." He indicated a fallen log almost under the tree where Frank had hidden. "Frank and Terry can tie up the big bad men over there."

"One of them has a lump on his head you wouldn't believe," Frank said as he stopped by the mercenary lying prostrate along the trail.

"I put it there with his weapon after I took it away from him," Terry said.

Joe helped Lauren apply an impromptu bandage made from his T-shirt. He wanted to say something to thank her. But every sentence he started just sounded like a cliché. What could he say to someone who had just saved his life?

"I was so—" He stopped. "I don't know what word to use."

"What are we talking about?" Lauren asked.

"When you got shot. When I thought you were dead." He looked away from her, his brow furrowed. "I thought, 'It's happening again. I've failed.' "

"Failed?" Lauren said. "I can't imagine you ever worrying about failing at something."

"There was someone—very close to me . . . When you got hit, it was like reliving the moment that I lost her. I felt so helpless."

"Now, that's something I *know* you're not," Lauren said with a smile. A special light was sparkling in her bright blue eyes.

He stared into her eyes for a long moment, then nodded. "No. I don't feel that way right now."

"What do you feel like?"

Joe grinned. "*Like getting the bad guys!*"

Terry examined the job he and Frank had done of tying the mercenaries to trees. "I think that'll do," he said, satisfied.

Joe approached them. "I've got a plan."

"I think I heard it already. It's called, 'Get the bad guys,' " Frank responded.

"Right. We return to Hammerlock's fortress. No one, but no one, is going to be expecting us to try a move like that." Joe's grin turned wolfish. "We'll catch them with their pants down."

"He's got a point," Lauren agreed, walking up to them. "And we have some weapons now, besides."

"Not only that," Terry added, "but they have a communications center there. And it just so happens that my dad taught me how to send and receive. Do you read me?"

"We're going to get rescued!" Joe said, beaming.

"Or at least call the police and marines and a planeload of psychiatrists for these loony tunes," Terry said.

Suddenly they heard a distant shout from deep in the jungle.

"Brand!" a voice shouted. Hammerlock's voice.

No answer came. All four of them listened, startled by the intrusion.

Finally Hammerlock shouted again from somewhere. "Brand! Forget the others! You're mine!"

The jungle went still again. They listened for a long while.

Biff made his way painfully over to the group,

limping. "Hey! Did you guys forget about me?" he complained.

Joe clapped his hands together. "Nope. We waited around just for you. Come on, it's time to move out and take over the fortress."

Biff looked from Frank to Terry to Lauren. "What's he talking about?"

Joe picked Biff up and slung him over his shoulder. "Don't worry. You'll love it!"

Dark clouds crept over the mountainside. They used the shadows from them for cover until they were close enough to take their first prisoner, one of the guards on the outer perimeter.

The man wasn't about to argue with two guns aimed at his head. He gladly handed his weapon over to Lauren.

No one had alerted the men in the fortress to be on the lookout, so it was relatively easy to approach them. They made their prisoner march ahead of them for cover and took new prisoners as they moved deeper within.

At last, they came to the stairs that led to the dungeon chambers.

"Terry," Lauren said, brightly, "how would you like to escort me as I show these model prisoners the latest in dungeon accommodations?"

"Sounds delightful," Terry replied.

Some of the captured guards turned to see if

they were joking. Terry and Lauren smiled and pointed the way with raised gun barrels. The prisoners all decided it would be a very good idea to check out the dungeon area.

"While you do that Joe and I will look for their communications center. It has to be somewhere on one of the upper floors," Frank guessed, looking about for the stairs that had taken them up to Hammerlock's inner sanctum.

Frank walked over to a high-backed chair and shifted Biff off his shoulders and into it.

"And what am I going to be doing?" Biff asked.

"Pretend you're the king," Joe suggested as he and Frank began to search the premises.

Biff waved the hand holding the machine gun. "With this, I guess I am."

The Hardys found the stairs. They searched room after room on each floor. Finally they found the radio room on the fourth floor. Two radio operators sat with headphones on, absorbed in the equipment in front of them.

Frank came up behind them and quickly jerked the headphones away. The two radio men turned to see Joe aiming the Super Blackhawk pistol in their direction; the seven-and-a-half inch barrel was a silent but imposing presence in the room.

"Recognize it?" Joe asked.

They tied up the operators with extension cords from one of the closets.

"Let's go find Terry and let him get this thing operating for us," Frank proposed.

Frank was feeling pretty good. They hadn't run into any real opposition. No one had been seriously hurt. On the way up the stairs he'd passed a mirror and for once, he had to agree with Joe. He *did* resemble a walking lump of oatmeal, but it seemed a small price to pay.

Then as they left the communications room they got lost.

They had covered so many corridors and gone through so many different rooms that somewhere on the route back they made a wrong turn. They realized it when they entered a long corridor, carved out of solid rock.

"I don't remember being here before," Joe said.

"Excellent deduction," Frank commented. They walked slowly down the corridor. It was dimly lit with a single sixty-watt bulb. The shadows they cast upon the clammy walls looked like elongated gray ghosts.

"Hello," a voice said from behind them.

Frank halted, glancing at Joe. "Did you hear that?"

"At least he didn't laugh. I really hate his laugh," Joe said, turning.

Brand stood at the end of the corridor they'd just come from. He held his machine gun at waist height.

"You ruined it all," he told them. His voice cracked with emotion.

"Brand!"

The voice calling Brand's name sounded exactly as it had in the jungle. But in those close quarters, echoing off the stone walls, it raised gooseflesh on Joe's neck. It came from behind them.

The Hardys turned the other way. Hammerlock stood at the opposite end of the corridor, covered with sweat, grease, and blood. His shadow stretched nightmarishly behind him.

"I told you, Brand. You have to answer to me," Hammerlock growled. His guttural voice sounded more animal than human.

Frank and Joe looked back and forth. They were caught between two murderous men. In seconds the dimly lit corridor would be filled with bullets—and so would they.

These rough-hewn rock walls could easily become their tomb!

Chapter

18

JOE SNAPPED HIS pistol up quickly and pulled the trigger. His target was the dim light bulb. When it shattered, the whole corridor went as black as the interior of a crypt.

The sound of the shot reverberated through the room.

The Hardys each dove for an opposite wall of the corridor, pressing against the cold stone. Sharp edges dug into their backs.

Rapid gunfire lit the blackness in sudden spurts from both ends of the corridor. Joe squeezed the trigger of his gun again. Click!

"Our cannon just ran out of ammunition," he whispered to Frank. "Now what do we do?"

Bullets ricocheted off the walls at the ends of the corridor.

"Let's go for Brand!" Frank whispered. Fortunately the racket of the gunshots kept them from being overheard by either of the men. "He's closer."

"And not as strong," Joe added.

They moved as quietly as they could along the corridor, trying to stay flat against the walls. Their luck held as the bullets continued to rip down the middle of the long hall.

The gunfire abruptly ended on both ends of the room, as if by some cue. With the absence of noise, the place became darker, more ominous.

Joe froze. He knew they must be close to Brand. But he couldn't even see Frank, who was only across the width of the corridor from him. He listened. Nothing, just silence as vast as the darkness. He could feel his hand growing sweaty on the heavy gun.

Brand cleared his throat.

The sound was so close to Joe that he almost jumped back. Instead, he flung himself into the darkness, trusting his ears. He rammed into Brand, both of them tumbling to the floor. Hammerlock heard the scuffle.

"Brand!" he shouted. "You want to know what I'm doing, Brand?"

The major whacked Joe with the machine gun in a desperate effort to get free. Frank managed to grope through the dark, guided by the sounds of struggle, and pried the weapon loose from Brand's hands.

"I'm putting on my light-intensification goggles, Brand! And you know what that means? It means I can see you in the dark. I can see your little friends! And you can't see me!"

Hammerlock's voice seemed to spur Brand into panic. His fists flailed wildly, but most of the blows he delivered glanced off.

"Ah, I see all of you. Having a good time down there?"

As Hammerlock's voice faded, they could hear him stepping quietly toward them along the stone floor.

"I'm going to have to kill you all," Hammerlock said. His voice sounded almost rational. *Almost.*

Frank managed to get a choke hold around Brand's neck. Gurgling, the man clawed at his hands. But Frank held tight. When Brand's arms went limp, Frank let go.

Joe jumped to his feet. "Let's get out of here!"

"My sentiments exactly!" Frank exclaimed.

They ran through the darkness, afraid that at any moment they might trip over some obstacle. Reaching the end of the corridor, they turned blindly. "Come on!" Joe called. He ran on for about ten feet.

Then he crashed into a wall.

"Dead end!" Joe said, as if he couldn't believe it. Desperately, he ran his hand along the obstruction. "Wait! A door!"

"Open it!" Frank urged as he caught up.

Joe's fingers searched for the knob, found it, and his hand slipped on the metal.

Locked!

"Ah! There you are!" Hammerlock said from somewhere in the darkness. "End of the game. I win."

"Break it in!" Frank shouted.

Joe hit the door with his shoulder. He yelled in pain. The door remained fast, but his shoulder felt as if it were broken in a dozen places.

"Not with your shoulder," Frank admonished. "Kick it in!" He came up beside his brother. "Together!"

They both kicked out at the same time, right at the door handle. There was a splintering sound, but the door held.

"Nice try," said Hammerlock, and his voice was frighteningly close in the dark.

They kicked again. Wood tore with grinding, splintering sounds. But still the door held.

"If you only knew how clearly these light-intensification goggles let me see your futile efforts." Hammerlock sounded as if he were right on top of them. "Of course, I could shoot you now. I could have shot you when I first rounded the corner. But I admire effort, even if it is hopeless. Too bad I'm going to have to call a finish to this little game."

They heard the click of a gun chamber.

"It really is the end of the game, you know," Hammerlock said matter-of-factly.

They kicked out again. This time, miraculously, the door rebounded inward, banging against the wall. Beyond were high windows, reaching to the roof, and through it the sun. The dark clouds had passed.

The Hardys blinked in the sudden brightness.

But behind them, Hammerlock screamed. "*The light! Noooooooo!*" The colonel clutched at the goggles, trying to rip them off. He dropped the machine gun he had been carrying.

The intensified sunlight seared through his eyes, incredibly brilliant. Bellowing in pain, Hammerlock tore the goggles off, crushing them in his big hands. He staggered around—arms groping—blind.

Joe walked up to the colonel, who was flailing desperately with his arms.

"Hammerlock?" Joe said quietly.

Hammerlock lunged for him. And missed!

Joe whacked him over the head with the butt of his gun. Hammerlock hit the floor. He didn't seem to mind that the floor was stone. He appeared to be asleep.

"Good night," said Joe.

Terry looked at the radio equipment and said, "No problem. Give me five minutes and I'll have this baby humming." He started flipping switches. "Who do you want to call to come and rescue us?"

"Some rescue," Biff moaned. "I'll be free only until I get home. Then I'll be grounded for the next nine years—if my father doesn't kill me first."

"I think your mother has first dibs on killing you," Joe said comfortingly.

He walked over and patted Frank on the back. "Well, Frank, you might be kind of a nerd sometimes, but you always come through in a pinch."

"Is Frank really a nerd?" Lauren asked, her eyes merry now that the danger was over.

"Well, he loves to play with his computer and he can't dance and he has no sense of humor at all," Joe replied. "Ask Biff."

Frank threw up his hands. "I don't know why I'm so misunderstood. I'm a fun kind of guy." He brushed his hand through his dark hair and saw that it came away covered with chunks of crusting mud. "Why should I get this flak just because I have superior intelligence?"

Joe brushed away some more of the dried mud from Frank's shoulder. "That's not flak. That's *flakes!*"

They stepped outside, onto the battlements of the old fortress. Sitting side by side, tied hand and foot, were Brand and Hammerlock.

The last rays of the sun threw alternate bands of orange and black over Hammerlock's face. He almost looked like a human tiger.

"Looks like your eyesight is back," Frank said.

"Oh, I recognize you." Hammerlock's voice was a low growl in his chest.

"Hey, lighten up, Colonel," called Joe from the doorway. "At least you're out here in the fresh air. The rest of your boys are locked up in the dungeons."

The hate in Hammerlock's eyes was terrifying. "Why do you leave me with this traitor?"

"To keep an eye on you," Lauren said. "I wouldn't trust either of you alone."

"The next sound you hear will be that of helicopters," Joe cut in, "coming to take old Orville here to jail. And as for you, Colonel—well, I don't know *where* they'll put you. Some kind of—"

"Enough!" Sweat broke out on Hammerlock's forehead as he wrenched against the ropes holding him. The muscles on his arms bulged, his snake tattoo writhed. Then, unbelievably, Joe, Frank, and Lauren heard a snap! The ropes tore loose from Hammerlock's wrists.

Frank and Lauren darted a glance at the doorway. None of them had thought to bring their weapons out there. They had thought the prisoners were bound securely.

Obviously, they had thought wrong. Hammerlock ripped the ropes loose from his ankles as if he were tearing the string off a parcel. He rose to his feet, eyes glittering. "Now we'll see."

Despairing, Frank went into a karate stance. No way could he stop this man mountain, not when Hammerlock was in this enraged state.

"Colonel, what about me?" said Brand.

Hammerlock's answer was a vicious snap-kick that left his ex-subordinate groaning.

In that brief moment of distraction, Joe darted inside the doorway. He stepped out again. Even in the gathering shadows, everyone could see the outline of a pistol in his hand.

"Hold it right there, Hammerlock," Joe shouted.

The colonel froze. "You think that popgun can kill me?" he said.

"It won't have to kill you," Joe said. "All it has to do is blow you off this wall. It's a long fall to the rocks down there." He gestured with the muzzle. "And don't think about jumping me. I'm just a little too far away."

Hammerlock glared around in frustration. Then his tensed muscles sagged as Biff came out to join Joe, his M-16 aimed and ready.

"Look what we just found," Biff said, holding out several pairs of handcuffs.

"Put them all on the colonel, here," said Joe. Again he pointed his pistol. "Colonel, on the ground, please. On your belly. Hands behind your back."

A few minutes later Hammerlock was trussed like a turkey. But Joe still wasn't satisfied. He had the colonel wrapped in so many layers of rope that he resembled a mummy.

"Don't you think you're overdoing it?" Frank asked as Joe tied the finishing knots.

"I don't want to go through this business ever again," Joe said.

"Why?" asked Lauren. "You handled it so well with that pistol."

"That's precisely why I don't want to do it again." Joe picked up the pistol, aimed it at Hammerlock, and snapped off a shot.

"*Joe!*" shouted Frank.

His cry almost drowned out the *pock!* of the gun. Then a smear of magenta paint appeared on the wall over Hammerlock's head. It dripped down on the colonel as he yelled in inarticulate fury.

Biff stared in disbelief. "That's a paint-pellet gun from one of their games!" he said.

"You bet it is," said Joe. "Now you know why I'd never want to face him down again with one of those."

He grinned, then turned to Biff. "And you can do me a favor, pal. Next time you take up a game, make it checkers."

Frank and Joe's next case:

Callie Shaw has had it with the Hardys! Frank's girlfriend wants to know why she can't work with them. She's just as good an investigator as they are.

Storming home after an argument, she literally walks into an ambush—and a deadly test of her detective abilities. As more and more mysterious attacks are aimed at Callie, one thing becomes clear. This case had better be solved before she gets killed!

With the help of a beautiful young investigative reporter, the Hardys tackle one of the strangest cases of their career. Will they find the mysterious attacker? Can they save Callie? Or are they in too deep even to save themselves? Find out in *See No Evil*, Case #8 in The Hardy Boys Casefiles.

HAVE YOU SEEN THE HARDY BOYS® LATELY?

THE HARDY BOYS © CASE FILES

- #1 DEAD ON TARGET 67258/$2.75
- #2 EVIL, INC. 67259/$2.75
- #3 CULT OF CRIME 67260/$2.75
- #4 THE LAZARUS PLOT 62129/$2.75
- #5 EDGE OF DESTRUCTION 62646/$2.75
- #6 THE CROWNING TERROR 62647/$2.75
- #7 DEATHGAME 62648/$2.75
- #8 SEE NO EVIL 62649/$2.75
- #9 THE GENIUS THIEVES 63080/$2.75
- #10 HOSTAGES OF HATE 63081/$2.75
- #11 BROTHER AGAINST BROTHER 63082/$2.75
- #12 PERFECT GETAWAY 63083/$13.75
- #13 THE BORGIA DAGGER 64463/$2.75
- #14 TOO MANY TRAITORS 64460/$2.75
- #15 BLOOD RELATIONS 64461/$2.75
- #16 LINE OF FIRE 64462/$2.75